THE
R-MASTER

THE
R-MASTER

GORDON R. DICKSON

J. B. Lippincott Company
Philadelphia and New York

Lines from Rudyard Kipling's "Rimmon" in *The Five
Nations* are quoted by permission of Mrs. George
Bambridge and Methuen & Co. Ltd., the Macmillan
Company of Canada Ltd., and Doubleday & Com-
pany, Inc.

U.S. Library of Congress Cataloging in Publication Data

Dickson, Gordon R
  The R-Master.

  I. Title.
PZ4.D553Rm   [PS3554.I328]   813'.5'4   73-13837
ISBN-0-397-00920-8

Printed in the United States of America

THE
R-MASTER

1

Naked under a thin sheet, being floated on an airborne grav table along a white and shining corridor to the injection room, Etter Ho grinned ironically at the gleaming ceiling. There was a quotation that fitted the situation.

> Daily, with knees that feign to quake—
> Bent head and shaded brow,—
> Yet once again, for my father's sake,
> In Rimmon's House I bow.*

Only it was not for his father's but for his brother's sake that he was here, no different from any ambitious little desk-bound mind gambling on bettering itself, blind to the beauty of a work-free existence on the open seas. His sibling, Wally, had bowed down long since in this particular House of Rimmon; now Etter was following

* "Rimmon" by Rudyard Kipling.

him, after twenty-four years of being obligated to no one. Now, at last, he was no better than any of the billions of other individuals who had spurned the chance of freedom on a Citizen's Basic Allowance to scurry after the manacles of occupation, position, and authority within the machinery that made possible their utopian Earth.

Et's mind was daybreak-clear. He, like everyone else requesting the Reninase-47 treatment, had been offered a tranquilizer during the injection process, but he had refused. All drugs—even aspirin—were things he shied away from, for the reason he felt that the mildest of them could blur the experience of living, at least slightly. And to be blurred, to be fuzzed up in his perceptions, to Et was like dying a little bit.

So, now. Whether the R-47 should do anything for him or not, whether it should raise his intelligence a few I.Q. points or drop it, he wanted to be fully aware when the change was happening to him. Even if freak chance should result in a severe loss of mental acuity, as it had with Wally, he wanted to be aware of that, too, when it came. Not that this was likely. The odds against it were literally millions to one, nearly as impossible as the equally freak chance of the drug stimulating him to supergenius. None of it mattered. All possible happenings, everything, must be secondary to his own right to *know*. That determination in him was his personal curse, his commitment, and his faith; it would exist as long as life was still in his body.

The automated floating table surface on which he was being transported swung abruptly into a right-angle turn. A new stretch of corridor ceiling unreeled above him— but not all the way. There was an abrupt stop, another 90-degree turn, and he passed through a doorway into a room where the ceiling was a soft green. A small room. He could see the tops of the walls surrounding him.

"So this is our patient?"

A hearty deep-bass voice.

"Let's take a look at you, Mr. Ho."

The thin sheet was whisked away. The soothing color of the ceiling became a glittering mirror. He looked up and gazed at himself and at the possessor of the hearty voice, a bulky shape, foreshortened by the angle of reflection, green-clad even to the face mask and head covering.

"Why the gown, doctor?" Et asked. "This isn't an operation."

The eyes above the mask moved quickly over Et's body. "Regulations, I'm afraid," said the bulky shape. Brown, thick finger's palpated Et's abdomen. "A bit overweight, aren't you?"

"Not that I know of," said Et. "I've got big bones."

He lay staring up at the self he saw in the mirror. It was like watching someone he had never seen before. Why? Of course. It was because this was the last time he might look at his own image with the understanding of the mind with which he had been born. Never again might he really see himself as he now knew himself to be.

So he studied what he saw—a tall stranger, with coarse black hair and oval face. The Polynesian ancestry showed in the smoothness of the flesh that overlaid his muscles and had led the physician into the mistake of thinking him fat. The cragginess of the northern European—those big bones he had spoken about—were hidden and made secret under the sleek Pacific flesh. Volcano interior under peaceful forest slopes. A trapdoor to hellfire and damnation beneath the blue of calm tropic skies, for three generations now. Great-grandfather Bruder, how easy do your bones lie, back in the cold and stony earth of the Alps, if they remember the bright beaches of your island Mission?

The physician's fingers were prodding, palpitating. They stopped.

"You're in very good shape, Etter," said the deep voice.

"Thanks, Jerry," said Et. "Good of you to say so."

The masked face, which had started to turn away from him, turned back.

"Jerry?" it said. "I'm Dr Morgan Carwell. Were you expecting someone named Jerry to treat you?"

"No," said Et. "Pleased to meet you, Dr. Carwell."

The eyes above the mask stared down at him.

"You've already met me, Etter," the physician said. "Just an hour ago, before your final examination. Remember?"

"I know. That's right," said Et. "I met a Dr. Carwell. Did you meet someone named Mr. Ho?"

Their gazes held each other.

"Sorry, Mr. Ho. They tell us it's good practice to use a patient's first name. I apologize. Now, please relax. We want you as calm as possible."

"I'm relaxed," said Et.

"Fine." Carwell turned away. "Now, you shouldn't expect to notice physical sensations as a result of being given the medication. Lots of people tell us they feel various kinds of reactions, but the best we can come up with is that these are just the result of their expecting to feel something. Still, if you think you sense anything, I want you to tell me—"

Still talking, he turned back to Et, moving so that even in the mirror his bulk hid his hands from Et's view. Et felt the momentary light pressure of something pressed against the upper bicep of his right arm, even as Carwell's voice continued quietly and steadily.

"—because, as they've probably told you several times over, that's the whole purpose of administering Reninase-47 under these strict conditions. We do have a blocking agent available in the form of the countermedication. But if we need to use that, we want to use it as quickly as possible, so as to do the most good. And since the action of R-47 is so free of sensation in the patient, any clue we can get is highly useful."

"Doctor—" began Et, then fell silent again.

"Very good, that's right," said Carwell after a second. He had checked his own talking immediately when Et had opened his mouth. "We don't want you to speak unless it's necessary to tell us something important. The reason we don't want you to talk, of course, is to keep you from distracting the physician in his process of observation. That's also why you have to lie there without your clothes on for some minutes after I've given you the medication, while I stand here staring at you. Any physical change at all in your overall appearance can be important. . . ."

Carwell's deep voice went rumbling on in a monotone that was obviously intended to be soothing. Et had been repeatedly cautioned to relax as much as possible after getting the R-47. He tried to do just that. There was no point in pretending that he had no concern at all about what might happen to him. No normal human being could play roulette with the chance of being turned into a high-grade moron without fearing the results of bad luck, even if the odds against that happening were very long indeed. And in Et's case, there was Wally: Wally, to whom it had happened just that way . . . Wally, who had lucked out.

2

Probably, Et thought, if Wally had never decided to try the R-47, Et himself would have lived out his life happily without ever thinking twice of gambling with a drug that might either expand or cripple his inherent intelligence. But Wally, to get back a woman he had lost— a woman who was not worth three days out of his life, let alone two thirds of a lifetime—had so gambled, and now the chain of resulting events had brought Et to this room in turn.

Wally had always been unlucky with women, thought Et. He was three years older than Et, but they looked alike enough to be twins, once they had become fully adult. So Wally had not even had the excuse that he was physically unattractive to the opposite sex. Because Et, the younger brother, had no trouble at all. He liked women, many women, and most of them liked him back. Wally somehow always began well, but all the girls he met from high school on seemed to lose interest in him after a short while.

It was some sort of reverse magic in him that always seemed to trip him up. Finally, he had met Maea Tornoy, who was bright—admit it, Et thought now, she was very bright—and for the first time there must have been something for Wally to blame his failure on, if after some weeks of seemingly ripening companionship his relationship with the girl had seemed to cool.

He was not intelligent enough to interest Maea, Wally must have concluded. So he had taken his physical exams and put in an application for the same R-47 treatment Et was taking now.

Afterward, when the first signs of a negative reaction to the R-47 had appeared, they had taken him to a pleasant, large, brick building surrounded by parklike grounds, on Hilo, where gentle-voiced people cared for him. The deterioration of his intelligence did not happen at once but came on by jumps; as soon as Wally had realized clearly the end condition toward which he was headed, he had hung himself.

Upon Et, who had been a lotus-eater all his life, Wally's death had come like a sledgehammer smashing into a tinsel dream. For twenty-four years Et had kept the world and Wally's view of it at arm's length, in spite of Wally's unceasing attempts to convert his brother to a realization that life was serious and the perfect-seeming world that surrounded them had serious problems.

Et had always known that to be a pipe dream—until now. So Wally had done battle with his serious world alone. He had taken it on until it had finally taken him out. The final result was that he had fallen for a girl who had pushed him to push the world even farther, so that he had taken the

R-47 treatment and had had the sort of one-in-millions tragedy that, it seemed, only befell the serious in any world.

But the hell of it was, the world *was* serious. At least in the sense that it was filled with serious people, people who took it seriously, as Wally had done. When Et was notified of what had happened, he had come back to find Wally tucked into a cryogenic capsule, requiring action by Et himself—he who had avoided action of any kind all his life.

Wally, he was told, had killed himself. True enough. But he had been found, cut down, and gotten into cryogenic stasis within minutes. It was possible that he could be revived and even possible, if the death shock had halted his R-47–induced mental deterioration, that he could be retrained and reeducated to live at least a relatively normal life.

"On the other hand, Mr. Ho," Et had been told by the physician in residence at the institution where Wally had died, "you should be fully aware that all this is only a possibility. The chances are just as good, or better, that your brother can't be brought back to functioning existence even if he has the best medical revivifying team available. And even if he is successfully revived, again the chances are strong that, rather than his mental deterioration having been halted by the death experience, he might be brought back with no mental capacity at all—in short, he might be no more than a human body in coma."

"Sure," said Et. He heard the tone of his own voice, dry and bleak. "But Wally would want to try, I think. What's the best medical team available for revivifying him?"

The physician looked embarrassed.

"That's another matter," he said. "I'm sorry if the way I mentioned the best medical team made it sound as if such a team was easily available. The best team in this sort of effort is a team gathered together by an outstanding specialist in cryogenic revivification, and all such specialists are literally booked years in advance."

"We'll make an appointment," said Et grimly. "Who's the best?"

"Well . . . actually, Dr. Garranto," said the physician.

Et touched the mincorder button on his wrist chronometer.

"Let me get that down. What's his full name?"

"Dr. Fernando James Garranto y Vega," said the physician. "But I have to impress on you that trying to get hold of Dr. Garranto is impossible. He specializes in unusual cases and never has any—"

"Wally's case isn't unusual enough?"

The physician flushed. He sat up in his chair.

"Forgive me," he said, "but I'm going to be very frank with you. Dr. Garranto is simply not available for ordinary cases. There are enough cases among the more important people in this world to keep him occupied full-time. Even if he took your name on a list, he'd never get to you. And if he did, believe me, you couldn't afford the operation."

"Now, wait a minute," said Et. "I may be on basic allowance, but I own an oceangoing sloop—"

"My dear Mr. Ho," said the physician, "if you owned a forty-meter yacht you might have trouble meeting the costs of such an operation. Do you realize what's involved? Not merely the mechanical requirements, which amount almost to the use of a small hospital in themselves, but the fees for a team of six to ten physicians, all experts in some particular area, from anesthesiology to terminal states, plus subordinate medical personnel."

"How much?"

"There's no way to tell."

"Give me an outside figure."

"There is no outside figure," said the physician. "I'll give you a minimum—three hundred thousand Gross World Product dividend units."

Et looked at him. He had worked for six years, more or less steadily, to buy the *Sarah*, as his sloop was named. She was worth at most fifteen thousand GWP units; and his basic allowance was under a hundred units a month.

"So you see, Mr. Ho," said the physician. "You see how it is."

But Et had not seen.

He was not ordinarily, or he had not been for the part of his life he could remember, someone to fly in the face of fate or scarify himself with determination to do the impossible. But Wally's death had reached deep into him and opened a trapdoor to something he had not consciously realized was there.

Through that trapdoor had sprung the flames of certain ancient, grim fires under the apparent blue skies and sunny beaches of Et's soul. Out of unsuspected volcano depths had come the fierce, righteous judgment of his Alpine fore-bears, to wake him as if from a lifelong lazy dream of paradise to the real existence of black sin and bitter penance. The world that, judging by himself, he had thought to bring nothing but song and laughter to any reasonable man had in fact brought lifelong sorrow, defeat, and final self-destruction to his brother. That world must repair the damage it had done in Wally's case—and in the same un-sparing, equal measure in which it had meted out its pain to Wally.

The full reaction had not come at once. It had grown as he had begun to check on what the physician had told him about the impossible means and costs of Wally's revival. The first assurance that the physician, if anything, had been understating the problem came from a Mr. Lehon Wessel, the local underofficial of the World Bank on Hilo, whom Et first consulted about arranging some sort of financing for the medical costs of the revivification.

"I'm afraid it's a problem," said Lehon Wessel. He was a thick-bodied long-legged man in his twenties with fair hair and fair skin that was burned red by the sun. His manner was soft and regretful. "Your assets and your income simply don't suggest the means to support the expense of your brother's operation."

"I know that," said Et impatiently. "I knew that before I came in here. But aren't there compassionate grants or special funds from the World Economic Council that could help me out or that I could draw on?"

Lehon Wessel smiled sadly.

"Of course there are such funds," he said, "but it's a complicated matter getting monetary support from them and to be frank with you, Mr. Ho, in your case any effort to do so would be wasted from the start. Such funds are intended to be available to the exceptional situation and the exceptional individual."

"If it's not an exceptional case to have a man commit suicide because of a bad reaction to R-47, what is?" demanded Et. "That bad a reaction's supposed to be just as uncommon as the freak good one that makes an R-Master from someone taking the drug. And how many R-Masters are there? One in a few hundred millions of people who try R-47."

"Of course," said Lehon Wessel.

"Well?" said Et. "Can I apply for the funds or can't I?"

"You can fill out an application," said Wessel.

He gave Et a thick sheaf of printout forms to be filled in. Et took them back with him to the hotel where he was staying and discovered that he was required to be an expert not only on his own personal history but on Wally's. He called up Wessel on the phone to protest.

"What is this?" demanded Et. "Ninety-nine percent of this information must be already available in our files in the World Economic Council's central computer!"

"Of course," said Wessel. "But regulations require that the applicant make out the forms. I'm sorry."

Et made out the forms, eventually, and put them in. After a wait of nearly two weeks, he was called in by a man who was Wessel's immediate superior.

"Mr. Ho, come now," said the superior, leaning across his desk to talk to Et with a frank and friendly smile, "you surely don't want to try to push through these requests for funds? It's not my duty to discourage any applicant, but in your own interest I have to tell you that your chances of success with this are practically nil. Assistance from these sources is reserved only for those obviously deserving."

"My brother isn't deserving?" Et demanded. "It was in an effort to make himself more useful to the world that he had the bad reaction from the R-47 that led to his suicide."

"Oh, of course—your brother!" said the other man. "But it isn't your brother who's the applicant. It's you. And to be frank, Mr. Ho, nothing in your life record shows any promise of value equal to the sum you want to derive from EC funds to revive your brother."

"What about Wally's value, once he's revived?"

"But we don't know he'll be of any value, Mr. Ho. Medical opinion is very doubtful of returning him to a useful state of mind and body. Of course, he'd still be deserving, except that he's presently in an effectively noncitizenship state."

"Then suppose I apply in his name?" said Et.

"I'm afraid that's impossible as long as you're of close relationship enough to be responsible. A sibling or a parent automatically becomes guardian for anyone in a cryogenic state where revival is possible. As guardian, you have to apply for aid on your own merits, not those of your ward."

"All right," said Ho. "Then I so apply."

The other sighed.

"If you insist," he said. "I'll put these applications of yours through. But I warn you not to expect very fruitful results. Why don't you see an ombudsman?"

"I will," said Et.

The forecast he had been given turned out to be correct enough; the application was refused. Et turned to an ombudsman, one of those individuals who were supposed to help the ordinary citizen in his tangles with official red tape, and found the ombudsman as pessimistic as everyone else had been.

"We can appeal, of course," said the ombudsman. "But . . ."

He shrugged.

They appealed to regional authority, were turned down, appealed again to a review board and were turned down, appealed once more to the Northwest Quadrant Court and were denied.

"We can go on," said the ombudsman to Et. "We can go on for years, of course. There's no end of appeals and requests for review you can make. But you could grow old at this, still getting nowhere. Etter, the problem is that you've never shown any potential social worth. You're like a man without a credit rating trying to borrow from a lending institution. Take my advice. Give up. Or—"

The ombudsman hesitated.

"Or what?" prompted Et.

"Or go out right now, find yourself an occupation, and start working your way up in the active ranks of society," said the ombudsman. "Possibly in five years, very possibly in ten, you'll have climbed to a position of social usefulness where funds will be available to you. Meanwhile, since he's in cryogenic suspension, the time won't mean a thing to your brother."

Et looked grimly across the desk at the other man.

"You don't really think I'll do that?" he said.

The ombudsman shook his head.

"No, of course not," he said. "But it's part of my job to point it out as a course that's open to you."

"I'm obliged," said Et dryly. "Because as a matter of fact I'm going to do just that." He looked at the startled ombudsman. "Maybe I can make it in less than five or ten years."

"You mustn't get your hopes up," said the ombudsman.

"It wasn't hope I was thinking of dealing in," said Et.

He left, saying no more to the ombudsman. Actually, he had been making his plans for some time. Clearly, if he was going to beat the masters of the red-tape jungle in which he was now lost, he must at least pretend to join their game But there was no reason not to use his own natural advantages in playing it.

As a very young boy, he had noticed that those who let their abilities show were pressured to use them. By primary school, he had learned to keep his score on intellectual capacity tests well below what it might have been if he had wanted to do his best. Wally, on the other hand, had not held back; Wally had consistently scored high—not genius level but not far below it. Secretly, Et knew himself to be at least his brother's mental equal, but he had a deep contempt for those who thought that intelligence alone could make them something remarkable among their fellow men and women.

The result was, he had an edge to play with. His final remarks to the ombudsman had been a deliberately calculated springboard. He would proceed from that announcement to take the same R-47 injection that had ruined Wally. It was a gamble, but a small one. The chance of two disastrous results from that drug in the same family must be statistically so tiny as to approach nonexistence. For the rest, a small loss in I.Q. would not matter much; a small gain would be all to the good.

The point was that having taken the drug he would have certified to the red-tape society his determination to make something of himself in social terms—plus the fact that afterward, by showing a good slice of his hitherto hidden ability, he could claim a rise in intellectual capacity from the drug, a claim no one could dispute. With that much to go on, plus bluff when necessary, simple hard work and a grim determination to take any means to power should move him swiftly up the social work-ladder.

In the end, he had no doubt he could get what he wanted for Wally, from this system that valued brains and position so highly. . . .

"*Mr. Ho.*"

It was Carwell talking. Et had almost forgotten he was still in the R-47 clinic, waiting for signs of effect from the drug.

"How do you feel now?" Carwell said. "All right?"

Et nodded.

"Well, then," said the physician, "the immediate period of reaction has passed. Let's get you back to the preparation room."

He reached out and touched the table controls by Et's head. The table rose slightly in the air and floated out the way it had come, the door to the corridor opening automatically before it.

"I'll come with you, of course," said Carwell.

He followed the programmed path of the table, back to the preparation room, where Et's clothes waited for him neatly on magnetic hangers.

"You still feel exactly the same?" Carwell asked.

"That's right," said Et.

"You can get up and dress, then," said Carwell. He watched as Et did so, asking once or twice if Et felt any reaction yet.

"I thought," said Et, as he pressed shut the closure slit on his shirtfront and prepared to leave the room, "you didn't expect any reaction."

"No physical reaction, of course," said Carwell. "But you might be noticing some mental alterations—anything at all, including mild hallucinations."

Et walked out. Carwell went with him, stripping the mask from his face as they both headed down a short stretch of corridor toward the lobby of the clinic.

"Not even those," said Et. He looked sideways at Carwell, who was fully as tall as he was and must weigh over a hundred and thirty kilos. "It's not taking?"

"Too early to say that," Carwell answered. "It's only a large percentage, not all, of our patients who show a reaction during the first few minutes after treatment. In fact, you must have been told by whoever talked to you before I did that there's no telling. Reaction can come any time, up to several weeks later, gradually or suddenly, any way."

"It seems to me," said Et, "I heard that strong positive reactions usually came suddenly, and soon."

"A majority of them, a majority of them," said Carwell. They were approaching the admitting desk, and the physician spoke to the nurse on duty there. "Mr. Ho's chart, please. I'll sign him out."

He turned to the white-clad male attendant standing by the desk.

"Looks like we won't need you, after all, Tom," he said. "Mr. Ho has had a fine uneventful response to treatment. Wait. On second thought, you'd better just walk with him to his car to make sure."

He turned back to Et and offered his hand.

"Well, Mr. Ho," he said, as they shook, "you'd better take it easy physically for the next twenty-four hours, just on general principles. Call us right away, of course, if you feel any unusual sensations, mental or physical. And check with me tomorrow at this time in any case. Don't feel discouraged, now, simply because nothing seems to have happened so far. In itself, that's a healthy sign as far as a negative response to R-47 is concerned. The longer you go without noticeable reaction, the better the odds on any reaction at all being a positive one. And as I say, don't expect results immediately. It's not at all unusual for nothing to be noticed for days, or even weeks."

"Sure," said Et. "Thanks, doctor. Thanks for everything."

He turned and went toward the door. The attendant fell in beside him.

"You don't really need to come out with me," Et said to him. "I'm parked so close you can watch me get into my car through the doors here."

"Orders," said Tom. He stepped a little ahead of him as they reached the glass wall fronting the lobby and pushed his hand out. The transparent door slid back silently. "After you."

"Thanks," said Et. "No—wait a second."

He stopped, turning to his left to look at the wall framing that side of the lobby's glass front. The wall was paneled in oak strips, and the varying wood colors under the lightly stained, highly waxed surface had caught Et's eye. It was unusual to find oak trim used so lavishly here in the Hawaiian Islands, these days when hardwood was precious. He stepped closer to look at a widespread multiple arch of darker grain lines on one light brown strip. The lines caught his attention strangely. Suddenly, they seemed to become three-dimensional, like terracing on a hillside, leading his eye away and back into an imaginary land. It was a land where the oak belonged, before the metal of man had begun to scarify the world. On one such naturally terraced hillside, the oak from which this strip came had once flourished, spreading its thick limbs parallel to the earth, as one of its kind might have done back before the tick of civilized time. Child of the four seasons and no other, it would have stood, in that prehistoric time, safe and enduring, a citizen of the ages under the clean skies of a day out of eternity. . . .

Aquamarine morning, the oak would have seen, above the turquoise slopes . . . sapphire noon . . . amethyst and citrine evening . . . topaz twilight . . . tourmaline into onyx night: diamond, moonstone, pearl. . . .

Colors whirled in his mind.

"Doctor!"

Far, far off, a corner of his busy mind registered the unimportant voice of the attendant calling, the hands of the attendant catching him, holding him upright.

"Doctor! Quick!" The distant voice registered alarm and excitement. Great excitement. "It's a positive, a big one! *Jackpot!* Hurry!"

Garnet, carnelian, sardonyx, cameo . . . singing with the colors of an imaginative power he had never felt before, rushing away on the dark tides of his thought into the past, he had no attention to spare for the ordinary little men and women about him.

Amber, serpentine, malachite, cat's-eye . . .

3

He woke in a wide nonhospital bed, a dark antique four-poster—no grav float—in a rose-carpeted, paneled bedroom that looked out through two wide, heavily draped floor-to-ceiling windows onto a broad expanse of green lawn rolling away to walks of crushed gravel among shade trees. The silence and peace around him was absolute, and the light outside was a clean, clear, dawn light—as if even the relatively unpolluted air of the Islands had been just recently washed by a rain shower.

He felt comfortable and alive. Well, not completely comfortable. He had a small headache, a little queasiness in the stomach, a little pressure in the bladder; but these were probably only faint hangover symptoms, pushing against the pleasant drowsiness of waking. His mind was as clear as the atmosphere, calm, at peace, and alert. Whatever had happened to him, he did not seem to be under any ordinary sedative; he would have felt the effect of such with the sensitivity of his long hatred for medications.

On the other hand, he felt no sudden, positive increase of intellect, no special sharpness of perception, no new swiftness of cognition.

Rousing fully, he got up from the bed, discovering himself naked under the covers, and went to try a door which let him into a bathroom with equipment equal to that of the bedroom. Shaved, showered, and evacuated, he came back to the bedroom, found his clothes, and dressed.

Still, no one had come to find out if he was still sleeping. He turned to the bedside phone unit and keyed the operator stud.

"Mr. Ho?" said a female voice immediately. "What can I do for you?"

"I don't know," he answered, looking down at the speaker. "Where am I?"

"Dr. Carwell and the clinic Chief of Staff, Dr. Lopayo, will tell you. They'd like to see you as soon as you feel like seeing them. Would you want some breakfast, meanwhile?"

"Yes," said Et, discovering hunger in himself.

"If you'll give me your order then, Mr. Ho."

He ordered orange juice, bacon, toast, and coffee, his mind at work on the situation now unfolding around him. He continued to think about it after the food had been brought in on a grav-float table by a dark-haired girl in a white but nonuniform dress, who merely smiled when he tried to open a conversation with her and went out again.

Certainly, thought Et, finishing up the last of his toast, what had happened to him had to be obvious. The luxury of his surroundings, the memory of the attendant shouting *"Jackpot!"* just before Et ceased to remember anything at all—these things alone were enough to justify believing he had achieved a really strong intelligence-increasing reaction to the R-47. It was too much to suppose that he had had one of those rare positive reactions to R-47 that resulted in a maximum increase in capability, up to the supergenius level. There were supposed to be only sixty-odd people alive in the world today in whom R-47 had produced such a reaction, as opposed to the two hundred or so who had, like Wally, suffered the ultimate in negative reaction.

There were three strong objections to hoping that he might have been so lucky. The first was that the odds against it were ridiculous, several million injectees of R-47 to one for each supergenius created. The second was that, if true, he would have to do some rethinking of his plans. He had hoped for, at the most, a mild increase in intelligence, since that was all he needed to convince the faceless officials of the Earth Council that he was a new man, a man they could lend to.

The third and most convincing reason against believing in any great benefit from the R-47 was that as far as any sensations went he felt absolutely unchanged. There were no great ideas suddenly exploding in his brain, or special new swiftness or clarity of thought. It was the same old brain in his head as far as he could tell, and he was the same old self.

There was a soft knock at his door. He frowned at it. No door chime? Or was it part of the antique surrounding, to avoid mechanical announcement of a desire to enter? And if so, why? The girl with the breakfast, come to think of it, had just slid into the room without any signal.

"Come in," he said.

The door opened, letting in three men. Carwell in a

white physician's coat, another older and leaner man almost as tall as the big doctor and also white-coated, and a short plump man somewhere in middle age, wearing matching jacket and shorts. He was almost hairless and had a pink, round baby's face. An ordinary man, this last one, but something stirred uneasily in Et as their eyes met.

"Mr. Ho," said Carwell, and there was no doubt about the politeness in his voice this time, "this is the chief of our R-47 clinic, Dr. Emmera Lopayo, and Mr. Albert Wilson."

Et got to his feet and shook hands with all of them.

"Mr. Wilson," said Dr. Lopayo, as they pulled up chairs and Et sat back down on the edge of the bed, "is Chief of the Accounting Section in the Earth Council. He doesn't ordinarily come to things like this—"

"I was in the islands, though"—Wilson beamed—"and since my section is responsible for people like you, Mr. Ho . . ."

He let the rest of the sentence go, as if there was no need to complete it. He was very friendly, but Et did not like him.

"It's an occasion for us, of course," said Dr. Lopayo. "I take it you understand, Mr. Ho?"

"You aren't telling me I'm one of the galloping successes of R-47 after all, are you?" Et said. "How sure are you?"

"Oh," said Carwell, "we're sure. How do you feel?"

"No brighter than I ever did," said Et.

"That's natural. Very natural," said Carwell. "But I was asking how you felt physically."

"A little creaky," said Et.

"Good," said Carwell. "Good. You can't do better than that."

"I can't?" said Et. "Maybe you'd better give me some more information about how R-47 works. I know you and the doctor who gave me my physical briefed me on it before the injection, but I don't remember that there was anything about how I should feel if I turned into an R-Master. Was there?"

"Not really," said Carwell.

"Come, Morgan," said Lopayo to him, "Mr. Ho is in a position to understand the whole process a lot better now. Besides, he can ask any questions he likes, and we've got an obligation to answer them."

"Not really . . . just yet," said Wilson, beaming. "Not until he's legally a ward of the Earth Council. We should get that out of the way first." He appealed to Et. "May I call you Etter?"

"He prefers Mr. Ho," said Carwell.

"I'm a public figure now, I guess," said Et. "Go ahead and call me Etter, if you like."

"Etter, you'd prefer getting the paperwork out of the way as soon as possible, wouldn't you?"

"What paperwork?"

"To confirm your new status." Wilson smiled. "You've got two choices, you know."

"Choices?" Et said. "Of what?"

"That's right." Wilson's smile was a constant. "You can choose to become simply a ward of the Earth Council or you can be a working citizen, with an Earth Council passport and extraterritoriality."

"What's the difference?"

"Just one thing—work," said Wilson. "As one of the unusually successful results of the R-47 program, you can simply live as you like, at EC expense, from now on; the Earth Council will shoulder all your life expenses. Or you can live as you like but also work for the EC, either at some problem we'd like you to attack or at something you choose yourself. As a ward of the EC, in the first place, you have complete protection and perquisites; as a worker, you have equal protection and perquisites, plus you'll be delegated whatever authority you need to do the work in which you're active."

The word "authority" in Wilson's voice seemed to ring with an almost reverent echo.

"I suppose I could choose a category now and change later?" Et asked.

"Oh, certainly," said Wilson. "Of course, later it might take some time and trouble to change over. Red tape, you know."

"I think I'd rather be a worker," said Et.

"Very good," said Wilson. He leaned over toward the phone unit on the table by Et's bed. "Send in Rico Erm with the papers. Rico will be your executive secretary," he added.

A slim young man in matched business shorts and shirt like Wilson's brought in a sheaf of forms, and Et was put to work signing them. He scanned each before he signed it and discovered that he was renouncing his ordinary citizenship, declaring himself a stateless person, petitioning the Earth Council for EC citizenship, and, finally, accepting that citizenship on a Class AAA level.

"Very good," said Wilson, when Et was through. "Let me be the first to welcome you to the ranks of EC personnel, Etter. Now, what would you like to do?"

"I'd like to find out how to go about getting the best possible medical team for revivifying my brother, who's in a cryogenic state at the moment."

"Oh, yes." Wilson turned briefly once more to Rico Erm, then back to Et. "I noticed that matter in your records, that you'd been trying to arrange compassionate funds for the revivification of—what's his name—Wally. Of course, you could afford to draw on your own credit as an R-Master for that now, if you wished. But there's really no reason why the compassionate funds shouldn't be used."

"There isn't?" Et asked.

"Of course not. Can you find that D7K1439 form there, Rico? . . . Ah, there it is." Wilson received from Rico a single sheet of paper which he handed across to Et. "These local officials! Still, you have to make allowances. There really are a tremendous number of forms and routes for a request to take. Just sign that, Etter, and the whole matter will be funded."

"What is it?" Et asked, glancing at the form. "Instant certification as a citizen useful enough to be entitled to compassionate funds?"

"Nothing so complicated," said Wilson, good-humoredly. "Just a waiver of responsibility in the case of your brother. Naturally, once you waive responsibility, he becomes the ward of society and entitled to compassionate funds for his rehabilitation on his own. Actually, this form was the only thing you ever needed. A shame the people you talked to didn't realize that."

"Yes," said Et. He signed and passed the paper back. "A real shame. By the way, there was a temporal sociologist my brother knew, whom I'd like to talk to. A Maea Tornoy."

"We'll locate her for you, Mr. Ho," said Rico Erm.

"Yes, well, we others have to be moving along here," said Wilson briskly. "Duties, Etter. Constant duties. Would you care to walk out to the aircraft with me, Rico? I can brief you on the way."

He led the other out of the room. As the door closed behind both of them, Et turned to the two physicians

"Good to have met you, Dr. Lopayo," he said. Both Lopayo and Carwell stood up, Carwell's hand going to the right-hand pocket of his white coat. "I hope we meet again some time. Dr. Carwell, I think we were going to have a talk."

Dismissed, Lopayo left. Carwell hesitated, still on his feet. As the door closed behind the clinic chief, Carwell brought his big hand out of his pocket, holding a small container of white pills about the size of aspirin. He stepped over and handed these to Et.

"What's this?" Et asked.

"An analgesic and tranquilizer of sorts," Carwell said. "To clear up any minor discomforts you may be feeling."

"Thanks, no," Et said. He tried to hand the pills back. "I don't like drugs. I'll put up with the discomforts."

Carwell avoided his hand.

"Please," said Carwell. "I'm required to give them to you. Besides, in the long run you'll find—I think you'll find that you want them, after all."

"Oh?" said Et. "We'll see."

Carwell was still standing. Et waved him back to a chair and sat down himself, putting the container of pills in his pocket.

"Now tell me about my new increase in intelligence."

"Well . . ." Carwell hesitated. "I'm not really the expert you want for that, Etter—"

"Et."

"Et. I mean, I've had the training to do the job I did in the R-47 clinic, but that's a long step from the handful of physicians who've specialized in the health care of R-Masters themselves. One of those will be assigned to you, and he or she can do a much better job of answering your questions than I can."

"You'll do for now," Et said. "Tell me what's happened to me. How much brighter am I?"

Morgan Carwell looked uncomfortable. He sat almost lumpily in the chair facing Et, a big brown man clearly struggling with himself.

"I don't even know if you should be told this just yet," he said, "but we're asked to answer any questions an R-Master asks. The truth of the matter may be you actually aren't any brighter at all. Or at least that's the best theory on the R-Master reaction at the present time."

"Not brighter?" echoed Et. He did not astonish easily, but he felt astonishment now. "I don't understand. You mean R-47 is some kind of fake? If that's so, how can I be an R-Master?"

"No, no," said Carwell hurriedly. "From a practical point of view, you might as well consider that you've had a raise in intellectual capacity. It's not that the effect isn't essentially the same; it's that we don't believe the mechanism creating individuals such as you've become actually raises their innate intelligence."

"Then what's the explanation?" Et asked.

"Well, if you order it, I can get you a number of books and papers on the subject," said Carwell. "Most of them are on the restricted list—not for you, I suppose. But some of them I haven't had EC clearance to read myself. I assume those just go a little farther into detail than the ones I'm acquainted with. To put the thing in nonmedical language, we think what happened in your case—and a few rare others—is like becoming highly sensitized to some allergenic substance. For some reason, in the case of a very,

very few people injected with R-47, the whole being of the person develops either an unusual sensitization to intellectual demands so that he immediately puts forth an unusual mental effort or he becomes desensitized to any and all intellectual demands." He coughed. "What's known as an extreme negative reaction."

"Such as my brother had," said Et grimly.

Carwell paused to look at Et almost appealingly.

"I don't know if I'm making myself clear," he said. "As I say, I haven't been trained to give this sort of explanation—"

"Just keep talking," said Et. "You haven't said anything yet I don't follow."

"Well," said Carwell, "as you probably learned in school, R-47 was developed about fifty years ago, around the beginning of the century, because in the twenty or thirty years before that—the last part of the twentieth century—medical science had begun to realize that we needed a whole new class of drugs, a class unlike the sedatives and stimulants and narcotics of the twentieth century, which often did more harm than good, which were capable of being addictive, and which lent themselves to being abused."

He paused.

"Go on."

"All right," said Carwell. "As they must have taught you in secondary school Personal Physiology classes, there was a tremendous push toward the end of the twentieth century to find a new class of more useful drugs. The search was for whole-body medications, not just chemicals aimed at a specific effect but variants built on the human body's own chemistry that would help in suppressing or exciting natural reactions. For example, nowadays we'd never think of putting into your system a chemical, organic or inorganic, intended directly to conflict with an inimical virus that was affecting you. Instead, we'd supply your system with Acorton-78, Myerese-17, or one of the whole-body–antibody stimulants."

Et nodded encouragingly.

"Well, that's it," said Carwell. "As you already must know, R-47 was an accidental discovery at a time when whole-body–antisleep stims were under investigation. Like a number of other drugs today, R-47 is a whole-body stim. Unlike other whole-body stims, however, its effect doesn't wear off. Once it produces its reaction in a subject, while the subject seems unaltered physically, he usually shows a heightened sensitivity to intellectual stimulation."

"An R-Master just gets a little more excited than all the rest when it comes to intellectual matters, is that it?" Et asked. "I thought I was going to be something more than that."

"You are," said Carwell. "That's the point. You Masters seem able to reach back into personal resources we wouldn't think you'd have. Put it this way. Ordinary subjects benefiting from R-47 can demonstrate remarkable feats of mental strength. But R-Masters can demonstrate the equivalent of hysteric strength, more understanding and conclusion than their tested intelligence ought to permit them to show."

"Then how can you be so sure their intelligence hasn't been raised?"

"It depends on what you mean by 'intelligence,' of course," said Carwell heavily. "But none of the tests we've developed for intelligence so far show an increase in the mental *capacity* of an R-Master, they just show greater speed and certainty in the perceptive and reasoning areas. And—one other thing—we've now had R-Masters as a result of R-47 for nearly fifty years. Not one of them has shown any real increase in creativity, let alone developed into anything resembling what's classically been referred to as a creative genius. If there's a flaw in a highly complex plan, a Master will spot it in minutes where it might take ordinary men and women days. If the solution to a problem is possible, the Master will find it in days where ordinary people would need months. That's all."

"Then why all the fuss about us?" Et said. "Why give us the best that the world has to offer just for being what we are?"

"Because you're valuable resources, of course," said Carwell. "And I suppose"—he hesitated a second—"because you represent a phenomenon that's still being studied."

"Ah," said Et. "So that's it. Guinea pigs."

"I'd guess that's a good share of it. As I say, you're asking me questions I'm not equipped to answer. A little knowledge is a dangerous thing. Your brother—"

He broke off.

"What about my brother?"

"Nothing," said Carwell. "I just mean there are drawbacks to any physiological state, even that of being a Master—but your assigned physician can explain those things better than I can."

"I'll take your explanation for now," said Et. "What drawbacks?"

"I"—Carwell was genuinely unhappy—"I'm not supposed to be telling you things like this."

"You're supposed to tell me anything I want to know or do anything I ask you to do," said Et. "Or is what I've heard about the privileges of R-Masters a lot of nonsense?"

"No. It's true enough. But—"

"Never mind the buts, then. What drawbacks?"

"Well," said Carwell, gesturing toward the pocket in which Et had put the pill container, "for example, that medication I just gave you, that you don't want. There are real side effects to the R-Master reaction on the human body. You'll find yourself changed."

"In what way?" Et asked.

"You may have some trouble sleeping."

"I never have trouble sleeping," Et said.

Carwell said nothing.

"I see," said Et, after a moment. "All right, I'll take your word for it. It just proves what I always felt about any kind of drug; none of them are any good. But I'll tell you one thing."

He reached into his pocket, took out the pill container, and set it on the table beside him. "Sleep or no sleep, I'm not going to be taking these."

Carwell still said nothing. Behind the physician, the door opened, and Rico Erm once more entered the room, carrying what looked like a narrow-banded wrist instrument on a tray.

"Pardon me, Mr. Ho," he said to Et. "But your staff is arriving and your personal physician is already here. He asked if he could speak to you and Dr. Carwell, both, before Dr. Carwell leaves."

"He can do better than that," said Et. "He can leave himself. Dr. Carwell is going to be my personal physician." He turned to look at him. "That is, unless Dr. Carwell objects."

Carwell started.

"You want me?" he said. "Oh, no! No—no, it wouldn't work."

"I'm sorry, Mr. Ho," said Rico. "But that's impossible. Dr. Carwell isn't qualified. Earth Council requires that you have a qualified physician in attendance at all times."

"He can be in attendance if he wants," said Ho, "but I want Dr. Carwell. How about it, Morgan?"

"I . . . I . . ." Carwell stammered. "Naturally, any physician would be fascinated to be private doctor to an R-Master. But . . . I've got my work here. And I do have a few private patients." He looked at Et, disturbed. "I'd have to think about it."

"Think about it all you want," said Et. "But the slot's open—at least for the next few days."

"Thanks. I . . . I don't mean to sound ungrateful—"

"You don't." Et waved him out of the room. "Go think about it."

"Yes . . ."

Carwell went out, blundering a little in his emotion, through the door his big bulk almost filled. The door closed, and Et turned to find Rico beside him.

"This is a somewhat more complex device than the ordinary wrist chronometer. It puts you in touch on a continuous basis with the Earth Council computer center," said Rico. "Will you put it on, please?"

Et did so. On his arm it looked deceptively ordinary. "How does it work?" he asked.

"Press the stem," said Rico.

Et did so. A small semitransparent figure like the holographic image of a seated Buddha seemed to form above the dial, and a tiny voice spoke to him from what seemed to be inside his right ear.

"At your service, Mr. Ho. What can Earth Council do for you?"

"Just testing" said Et.

"Very good, Mr. Ho." The figure winked out. Et reached up to touch his right ear as if to locate the voice.

"You hear through a direct beam broadcast from the wrist instrument into your right ear," said Rico. "You're a valuable property, Mr. Ho. The Earth Council wants to serve you and protect you."

"I see," said Et, in a voice he hardly recognized. A cold feeling trickled down his back. All his life he had prized his independence. He had been watched over by no one since he was fifteen years old. Suddenly he felt like a dog on a leash.

"So," he said, still in that voice that was strange even in his own ears. "All right, what are my restrictions? Tell me now."

"No restrictions, sir," said Rico. "The wrist instrument is only for contact purposes. You know all men and women are free nowadays, and an R-Master is even freer than anyone else. There aren't any restrictions on you, Mr. Ho. You can go anywhere and do anything you like."

"Fine," said Et. The cold feeling was still working in him. "Let's try that out. I want to eat at the Milan Tower."

"Yes, sir," said Rico. "Eat at the Milan Tower, Milan, Italy. What time, sir? What day?"

"Today," said Et, chilling with the cold anger now enveloping him. "Right now. What'll it be—lunch time there, when we arrive? I want to have lunch in the Milan Tower, and I don't give a damn how you arrange it. You said I could go anywhere and have anything I want. Get this for me!"

4

"Yes, sir," said Rico quietly. He turned toward the door of the room.

"What do I do, call Earth Council about it?" Et asked.

"No, sir," said Rico. "I'll take care of everything."

He went out.

Left to himself, Et shuddered like someone coming out of icy water. The fury was passing from him now, leaving its inevitable residue, a sick feeling at the pit of his stomach. Years ago he had trained himself out of a boyhood temper as touchy as frozen dynamite, because of the internal reaction that followed after he let it explode. Always after giving way to the furious anger buried in him, Et felt befouled and depressed. It was not like him to lose his temper with someone not responsible, such as this Rico. Like a chime of warning in his mind, he suddenly remembered Morgan Carwell cautioning him that there were drawbacks to the physiological state of being an R-Master.

So, perhaps he would now have to conquer his temper reaction all over again—but he firmly intended to go on being the self he had always been by choice, in spite of them all. He would learn self-control.

Rico came back in.

"Ready to go, Mr. Ho," Rico said.

Et looked sharply at the smaller man. He had expected Rico to produce something startling in the way of results, but this was almost too startling.

"Already?" he asked.

"Your own aircar is in readiness whenever you are, of course," said Rico. "And I chartered a commercial line's intercontinental out of Hawaii port. Normally, there'll be an EC intercontinental on standby near any permanent residence you occupy. Your island's got one."

"Island?"

"There've been several estates set up for occupation by new Masters, until they can decide on whatever residence they prefer. The one available for you right now is a small man-made island in the Caribbean. I was about to suggest that we move there, but you asked me to set up lunch for you at the Milan Tower. Possibly after lunch you'd like to go to your island?"

"We'll see," said Et.

The intercontinental fell skyward, the effective three-gravities drive of her particle engine reduced by a two-grav internal interference to a practical single gravity under which Et could walk around.

Walk around he did. It was strange to prowl the empty transatmosphere ship, past the rows of easy chairs and lounges, knowing he was lifting above Earth, to glance into empty suites and conference rooms. He dropped into a chair and considered what this transportation was probably costing the Earth Council. Half loaded, at a fare of eighteen Gross World Product dividend units per passenger, this ship in a commercial flight would take eighteen thousand GWP units—which was possibly a little over the cost of the flight in materials, salaries, and depreciation of craft but not much over.

White-winged as a cloud under the blue sky of day, the *Sarah* sailed into his mind's eye. Sloop-rigged and clean-hulled, she came up into the blue mirror of a small bay, turned on her heel, and slid in to tie up at the dock below the large establishment where Wally had lived those last few months of his life. In this fashion Et had sailed in, the day of the radio message that had told him of Wally's suicide, and Alaric had been left with the *Sarah*, docked now at a marina on the big island. As far as Et knew, Alaric and the boat were still together there. It occurred to Et that he should get in touch with Alaric and tell him that the *Sarah* was all his. Alaric would not want to take her, but—Et grinned a little bitterly to himself—as long as he put it that Alaric was the only one who could be trusted with the boat, Al could not very well refuse. Not that in the long run he had ever refused to do anything Et had wanted him to do. Al was a born follower.

Nostalgia, so sudden, strange, and fierce it was like a shark knife going in just below Et's heart, stabbed at him suddenly. God, he had had all that once: *Sarah*, and all the blue oceans of the world, and freedom. Now here he was, suddenly an empty rich man, spending more in forty-five minutes on a whim than his previous basic allowance could have paid back in a couple of lifetimes.

Ninety-four dividend units a month subsistence allowance from the GWP, and *Sarah*. . . . He had worked and sweated for eight years to get the boat, but after that there had been nothing more he needed. He had intended to let the self-busy world spin its neat wheels and forget him. Ninety-four units, the minimum adult's basic allowance, kept him in sails and supplies. If there was anything else he needed, a day or two of work here or there supplied it. Women liked him, and he felt no need to father children who might put him under obligation to society and the population balance. Five more years without progeny and he would even be eligible for a bachelor's bonus.

He had felt safe, contented. Secure but independent, in a world where all things were good anyway. Even fifty years ago, he would have had to struggle for a living, perhaps, or risk his life in a war. Today there were no such problems. For half a century the world had been able to turn all its productivity to improving the human lot. . . .

He shifted irritably in the lounge chair, his eyes still closed. What was wrong with him? Perhaps this was one of the side effects of the R-47 about which Morgan Carwell had been about to tell him. He must make it a point to see that someone came up with that information right away. When he had sat down and closed his eyes Et had expected to nap without difficulty. That was how it had always been with him. But now . . .

Alaric. He was remembering the first time he had ever met the little man. The *Sarah* had been . . . where? Put in at some small Pacific island. There had been a number of boats tied up at that dock, not family or pleasure boats but honest tramps like the *Sarah*. He and some of the other boatmen had gotten to fooling around with boxing gloves, that was it.

That was when Alaric had appeared. Et had boxed in secondary school, and he had fast reflexes. He was not really good, not even a good amateur, but for someone who knew

very little about it he was not bad. He had been successfully taking on everyone from the other boats and even
some of the local people who were down on the dock.
Then, from somewhere—he was not one of the island people—had come this kid, this young man, younger looking
even than he actually was because of his shortness and his
round, open face. Somehow, Alaric had ended up putting
on the gloves with Et.

It had been ridiculous. The giant and the midget. But
only until they started. At first Et could not believe it. Al,
of course, was in no way able to hurt him, even on the rare
instances when he got past the great length of Et's arms
with something resembling a punch. Nor did Al know anything about boxing. That much was plain. But on the other
hand, Et himself could not touch the smaller man.

It was incredible at first, and then it became funny. Et
ended up laughing so hard at himself he could hardly move
his gloves. Without his shirt Al showed himself to be
solidly built, not a narrow target. But if Et's reflexes were
good, Alaric's were blinding. For all Et's knowledge and
natural advantages, he could neither corner Al nor lay a
glove on him. Roaring with laughter, he ended up making
roundhouse swings at the smaller man.

Al had not laughed back. Ducking, hitting out, with his
mouth a tight line, Al continued to fight and would not
stop until Et finally managed to grab him with both arms
and toss him over the side of the dock. Al came swarming
up the ladder, dripping with water, still ready to do battle,
and was only stopped by the surrounding crowd and the
fact that Et had sat down, taken off his gloves, and refused
to stand up.

That had been . . . what? Five or six years ago. From
then on they had become friends. Et had no desire to lead

anyone, but Al was a natural follower and in his own way as successful with women and the casual life as Et himself. There was nothing to bother either one of them until Wally . . .

They had both been running away from the world, thought Et.

The shock of that thought made his eyes open.

It must be the R-47, he told himself. He would never have come up with such a sour view of their way of life before.

A chime sounded through the ship.

"Landing in three minutes at Milan port, Mr. Ho," said the voice of Rico Erm from one of the walls of the lounge.

The Milan Tower, four hundred and twenty stories above ground, was currently the tallest building in the world, so narrowly tall that its needle shape could not have existed even thirty years before, when technology had not yet developed to the point to permit such structures. Massive grav plates between the stories counteracted the tremendous vertical load on its base; in addition to this, at the two hundredth and four hundredth floors it was horizontally steadied by four huge particle engines, automatically responding with drive thrusts to counter wind pressures that otherwise would have snapped the high tower like a breadstick.

Under the light of the Milanese sun, the top twenty stories of the tower swelled out into an elongated, transparent bubble without interior floors, a tall open space within which swam and floated grav-balanced platforms that were separate dining pads done in different decors. Their combined capacity for diners was something like five thousand people being seated and served at once; no more than forty-five minutes from any intercontinental pad on the face of Earth, the Milan Tower was the most popular lunch spot on the globe.

"Who do you recognize?" Et asked Rico. He had ordered the other man to join him for lunch, and they were at a table on a dining pad momentarily floating high in the bubble, so that they could look out and down over its edge on at least half a dozen other dining pads.

"Recognize?" Rico echoed.

"That's what I said."

Rico glanced around the pad they were on.

"I know the two security guards at the table to our left and the three in the dining pit behind you," said Rico.

"Oh?" said Et. It had not occurred to him that he might be guarded. "I'm the reason they're all around us?"

"Yes, Mr. Ho," said Rico. "You can choose later whether you want to be protected or not, but with a world population of six billion, there are always fanatics—"

"All right, never mind that," said Et. "I'm not interested in guards. I wanted you to tell me who you recognized among the other people on this pad, and on any others near enough to see, who're here for reasons having nothing to do with me."

"Yes, sir." Rico scanned the other pads nearby. "I don't see anyone I know personally."

"Recognize was the word I used."

"Yes, Mr. Ho. As far as just recognizing public figures or people who've been in the public eye, there're a lot of those around. Li Ron Pao, the Conductor of the Berlin Symphony, is just five tables over to your left. The Secretary of the Economic Council, George Fish, is the heavy man in the center of that party near the edge of the pad rising up level with us. There are several stage and screen people on the same pad. Marash Haroun of the First Holographists Mentality is on the other pad just beyond and below."

Rico went on. As their own pad changed position, coming into close proximity with other pads, there were more and more newsworthy or famous figures to identify. Et sat listening, studying each new person Rico named through half-closed eyes. Finally, Rico began to run down. He hesitated and interrupted himself.

"I can go on like this as long as we're here, Mr. Ho," he said. "Do you want me to?"

"No," said Et. "That's enough for the moment."

"I don't understand," said Rico. "Why do you want me to point out people you probably know as well as I do?"

"Because I don't," said Et.

"Don't?" Rico stared at him.

"That's right," said Et. "It appears I've been living a particularly quiet and sheltered life. I don't know most of the people who make this world turn."

"All men and women make the world turn," Rico said. "These are just the fortunate few whose work puts them in the public view."

"Mere toilers in the vineyard," said Et.

"Yes, sir," said Rico.

"Who just happen to be able to get reservations for lunch, like me, at the Milan Tower on a moment's notice."

Rico flushed. It was a curious display of emotion. Et would have sworn the other man was too self-possessed to show any expression.

"Tell me, Rico," said Et. "Who's the most important person in the world?"

"There's no *one* important person, Mr. Ho, you know that," said Rico. "Every man and woman is equally important to society, and that's the way it's been since the Earth Council was formed in 2002 to eliminate national rivalries and criminal activities. Everybody does what he wants—and doesn't have to do anything if he doesn't want to. The result has to be a world of sane people doing the work they do only because it's the work they most want to do. In a society where every man and woman works only for the sake of working, how can any one person be more important than another?"

"Unless he's an R-Master," said Et.

"An R-Master," said Rico, "has unusual value. But until someone like you, Mr. Ho, or the Earth Council, finds a use for that value, it's like a fine piece of art stored in a closet and forgotten. On the other hand, I fill one busy day after another with my own work. You are certainly more valuable than I am. But if I had to choose as to importance between one human unit and another, I'd have to say that at least for the moment I'm no less important than you and maybe more."

"Interesting," said Et, looking at the other with new curiosity and some respect. "Sometime you and I ought to talk at length—"

He broke off, turning his head sharply to look across to another pad which had just floated up level with their own. The corner of his eye seemed to recognize a familiar face, and now that he looked directly toward it he saw that the familiarity was no mistake.

"I was wrong, Rico," he said. "I thought I wouldn't find anyone here I recognized myself. But I do. That's Maea Tornoy over there."

"Maea . . . Tornoy?" echoed Rico. "I don't know the person. You mean the redhead in her twenties or thirties with—"

He broke off. Et looked sharply back at him.

"That's right. With the tall dark man and that particularly beautiful black-haired girl. Do you know them?"

"The man's Patrick St. Onge," said Rico.

"And the black-haired girl?"

"I—don't believe I know who she is."

"Who's St. Onge?" Et asked. "I suppose I should say, what's St. Onge?"

"An auditor, Mr. Ho. For the Earth Council. Auditors are responsible only to the Accounting Section Chief."

"You mean Wilson?"

"Mr. Wilson, yes," said Rico. He looked at Et a little strangely. "You certainly know that the EC Auditor Corps has the responsibility of uncovering and arresting offenders against the guidelines of the GWP forecasts."

"No. How would I? I've lived on minimum subsistence all my life."

"The work of the EC auditors is necessarily classified under Security," said Rico. "It's good manners not to refer to the fact that a person is an auditor."

"Oh?" said Et. "As an R-Master, how do I rank compared to an auditor?"

Rico laughed a little. "Of course there's no such thing as rank," he said. "But naturally, there are always people capable of being trained as EC auditors, and the few R-Masters in the world are the result of accident."

"Fine," said Et. "Do me a favor. Step over to those three people and ask them if they'd do me the kindness of joining me at my table. Explain that I'm a brand new R-Master and that the occupation of an EC auditor fascinates me."

Rico half got to his feet, then hesitated.

"Mr. Ho," he said. "If I might suggest—"

"Don't suggest," said Et gently. "Just do it."

Rico nodded, straightened up all the way, and went off to a corner where small floating aircars nuzzled the edge of the dining pad, waiting to convey diners from the pad to the elevator at the base of the bubble or from pad to pad. A second later, Et saw him in one of the cars, sliding across through the open air to the pad at which Maea Tornoy sat with Patrick St. Onge and the unknown girl with the black hair and the face of a cameo beauty.

Rico landed on the outer pad and approached the three. Before he was quite to the table, though, Maea stood up abruptly and left the other two, hurrying off in the opposite direction from that in which Rico was approaching, so that when Et's executive secretary reached the table only the two were left there. Et watched as Rico stood and spoke to them and their heads turned in his direction. He smiled and beckoned. Their heads turned back to Rico. There was a little more conversation, and then, somewhat slowly, they both got up and followed Rico back to his aircar.

A few seconds later, Rico had them at Et's table and was introducing them.

"Mr. St. Onge, this is Mr. Etter Ho," said Rico. "Miss Cele Partner, Mr. Ho."

"Good of you both to come over and talk to me," said Et, when they were seated around the table. "I wouldn't have imposed on you, but I saw you were friends of Maea Tornoy—"

"Tornoy? Was that her name?" asked St. Onge, looking at Cele Partner. He glanced back at Et. "I'm afraid I hadn't met her before today, myself."

"Maea," said Cele Partner, in a soft voice as attractive as the rest of her, "was working on the societal impact of deep-level gold mining in the Philippines at a time when

I was there, and we got to know each other. I ran into her today in Lucerne and brought her along to lunch with Patrick."

"But she's an old friend of yours?" St. Onge asked Et.

"Of my brother's. He's dead," said Et. He smiled at both of them.

St. Onge smiled back. He was a lean, handsome knife of a man with a level mouth and level dark eyebrows over shadowed eyes that seemed as devoid of depths as the eyes of a hawk or an eagle.

"It seems something almost like a misunderstanding that brought us together," the auditor said.

Cele Partner, who was sitting between St. Onge and Et, reached out and laid a hand gently on Et's arm.

"I wouldn't have missed the chance to meet an R-Master on any terms," she said. "There's only a handful to begin with, and they seem mostly to be recluses. I can't get over just sitting here with you like this. Tell me. What's it like, being an R-Master? What does it feel like?"

"Truthfully," said Et, "I haven't been able to notice any difference in feeling so far."

He smiled back at her. It was not the first time a woman had taken an immediate interest in him, but something inside him stood on instinctive guard in the case of Cele Partner. He felt, for what reason he could not say, that the interest she showed was not to be counted upon. At the same time, the touch of her hand, the scent of her perfume, and her startling beauty stirred him and made him breathe a little faster and more deeply in spite of the instinct for caution inside him.

"Tell me about yourself—about yourself before you took the R-47," she was saying.

And he was complying. . . .

5

It was probably an hour or more, but it seemed like only a few minutes, before Patrick St. Onge reminded Cele that it was time for them both to leave. The dining pad around Et seemed to become sterile and dull with their departure. He looked across the table at Rico, wondering how much the secretary had read of Et's inner reactions to Cele, but there was no sign on the other man's features to show he understood that anything more than a polite and pleasant lunch-table meeting had taken place. Before the R-47, Et would not have wondered if Rico had seen and understood too much about him. For one thing he would not have cared; for another, he would not have expected to be swept off his feet by any woman. Now, however, he was changed; and also, he reminded himself, he had never run into anyone like Cele before. He had not, in fact, imagined that a woman like that could exist in real life.

Almost she had made him forget all about Maea and his original reason for taking the R-47. He shook the thought of the black hair and cameo face out of his mind with an effort. He had had some reason to come here. . . .

Oh, yes, it had been to see what the uppermost part of the social body was like, that upper part he had always ignored but now was going to have to live with, since he had become a part of it. It had also been to test the extent of the demands he could make on the funds and services of the Earth Council. Evidently, he had not stretched things to the limit. Perhaps he could try pushing a little farther.

"Now," he said to Rico, "I'd like to go to Hong Kong for a little gambling."

"Yes, Mr. Ho," said Rico.

Less than an hour later, they were in another intercontinental—but a smaller craft this time, one bearing the EC emblem on it, an Earth Council courier ship. There was less empty space to roam, and after a short tour Et found that he did not really feel like roaming. He was slightly dizzy and there was a small headache behind his eyes which would not go away, together with a general physical feeling of cranky uncomfortableness.

He sat down in one of the seats and closed his eyes. After a while a small sound near him made him open them again, and he saw Rico in the act of putting down on the service table beside him a glass filled with some yellowish liquid that effervesced slightly.

"Try this, Mr. Ho," Rico said. "It should make you feel better."

"What makes you think I'm not feeling all right?" demanded Et.

"Merely a guess," said Rico. "You had a bit to drink at lunch."

"To drink?" Et stared at him. He had had two cocktails and part of a bottle of some sparkling German wine, which he had divided with St. Onge and Cele Partner; Rico himself evidently did not drink. "What are you talking about? I've handled half a liter of rum between six P.M. and midnight and still gotten up at dawn to take my boat across open ocean without trouble."

"Yes, Mr. Ho. No doubt. But that was before you had the R-47."

Et glared at the secretary. But even while he glared he had to admit that what he felt now was at least very like the few rare hangovers he had had.

"All right," he said at last to Rico. "Even if there's something to what you say, I don't like medicines."

"It's only an analgesic," said Rico.

"I said no." He closed his eyes again.

There was a faint sound. When he lifted his eyelids once more, a few minutes later, the glass had been taken away.

He tried to sleep. But again, as on the intercontinental from Hawaii, the easy slumber he had been used to all his life would not come to him and he barely dozed, fitfully dreaming of people half seen, of voices half intelligible which demanded things from him in urgent tones. It was almost a relief when Rico spoke to him again.

"We're landing in a minute or two, Mr. Ho."

The most elaborate gambling establishments of the mid-twenty-first century were maintained in and about what had been the old British crown colony of Hong Kong, as were the best-supplied stores and the most expensive health clubs and spas. It was a place to get rid of dividend units, pure and simple.

The biggest and most famous of the gambling establishments, which included stores, health clubs, and hotel and restaurant space merely as sidelines, was the Sunset Hut, a construction of innumerable levels built up around the 280-meter-high Sunset Mountain on Lan Tao Island.

Et checked into a suite of rooms in the hotel section of the Sunset Hut and tried once more to nap, but without success. At two in the morning, a good hour for gambling rooms to be active, he gave up and got dressed again.

"Did you arrange for credit?" he asked Rico, as they took the elevator to the roulette room.

"Yes, Mr. Ho," said Rico.

"How much credit have I got?" Et asked.

"As much as you need," said Rico.

"Unlimited?" Et looked at the secretary.

"For all practical purposes," said Rico.

"Well," said Et, "we'll see."

The roulette room, when they got to it, was a specialty of the Sunset Hut. It was the size of a large ballroom with a dozen transparent roulette wheels ten meters in diameter, one above the other, rotating two meters apart on a single vertical shaft. It was possible to bet the numbers on one wheel in the ordinary fashion, or on more than one wheel. A tote board on each grav chair kept track for the individual player. The ultimate bet was on a series of numbers to come up in sequence on all twelve wheels.

Et found himself a floating grav chair and took it up to the top level, to a spot where he could look down through all twelve wheels. He began to bet sequences on all the wheels. He bet heavily.

The perversity of luck ran true to form. Et, who had come just to see how much money the Earth Council would let him throw away, began by winning; because the odds on sequences were very large, he won ridiculous amounts. So ridiculous were the amounts, in fact, that at the end of a couple of hours of play a rumor began to spread through the Sunset Hut that he might in fact break the bank in the roulette room.

The local gaming laws forbade that he should be able to break the Sunset Hut as a total entity. Other gamblers in other rooms had to be protected in their own right to win. But the bank in the roulette room was estimated to be worth more than the combined total of the banks in all the other gambling rooms combined.

Et played on and won.

Then lost.

Then lost again. The tide of his luck had turned. His winnings melted away before him as he continued to play the house limit on sequences. Soon he was several hundred GWP units into his credit balance.

At that point his luck burned again; once more he won. But this time the run was short-lived. It broke and he started to lose once more, and from then on he lost steadily until he was over a million dividend units in debt.

Et leaned back in his grav chair. Beyond the one transparent wall of the room that looked outward from the mountainside, the day had dawned some hours since. His eyes were grainy, the headache behind his eyes a solid, malignant entity, although he had drunk nothing more than coffee since Milan. He felt more deeply exhausted than he could ever remember feeling before. He turned to Rico, sitting in another grav float beside him and looking as if they had begun their travels together only an hour or so before.

"Well," said Et, "what about it? Should I take my losses and quit, or should I try to win it back?"

"That's entirely up to you, Mr. Ho," said Rico. "Shall

I order another release of credit to you?"

Et gave up. Apparently there was no end to the funds the EC was willing to supply him. If he had felt even a little less exhausted, he might have tried their willingness a little further. But now all he wanted was the chance to sleep.

"Let's quit," he said.

He took his grav chair down and escaped from the swarms of other gamblers who wished to commiserate with him, apparently finding some magic even in a loser, provided he was a loser on a grand scale. He and Rico, accompanied by four inconspicuous men whom Et had learned by now to identify as more of the security personnel the EC had set about him for protection, took the elevator to their hotel suite.

Before they reached their floor, however, a strange, perverse thought took possession of Et and made him jab at random into the column of studs directing the elevator to the different areas of the Sunset Hut.

"Mr. Ho?" said Rico questioningly.

"Changed my mind," said Et. "Let's wander around a bit before folding up."

The elevator doors opened before him, and he stepped out into a plain metal-walled corridor. Rico was at his heels.

"I don't mean to object," said Rico. "But while the Earth Council has a tremendous amount of authority and even more power of good will, absolute protection for you, Mr. Ho, is something no one can guarantee—"

He broke off. A door a little way down the corridor ahead of them had opened and a man dressed in a tight-fitting suit of black, with a hand-laser clipped to his belt, had just stepped out. He caught sight of them and frowned.

"What are you doing here?" he said. "I don't see any passes."

"Mr. Ho is a new R-Master—" began Rico swiftly, but the man in the black suit cut him off.

"I don't care who he is. This is a private section. Get back to the elevator and get out of here."

Et grinned. He had been feeling miserable for hours but here was a situation that sounded like a possible fight, and the adrenalin suddenly pouring into his bloodstream was washing the weariness and the headache out of his awareness. He felt better than he had for hours.

"What's in that room you just came from?" he asked the man in black.

"Mr. Ho—"

"Never mind, Rico," said Et. "The man can answer me. Let him."

"I'll answer you," said the other. He reached back and touched a point on the wall beside the door. A high-pitched humming filled the corridor. The door opened and two other armed men in black came out. Farther down the hall another door opened to let out three men, and Et heard yet another door opening behind himself and his security men.

The security men moved forward. All at once, Et found himself surrounded by their bodies.

"Mr. Ho—may I?" Without waiting for an answer, Rico reached for Et's right wrist and lifted it to his lips, pressing against the stem of the watch-shaped communicator. The small holographic Buddha image appeared above the dial. "This is Rico Erm, speaking for Etter Ho. Security problem."

The men in black, who had been moving in, stopped. Rico let Et's wrist fall and stepped out from among the security men. With a coolness Et would have never suspected he possessed, the secretary walked up to the first man in black.

"From this point on," he said to the other, "Mr. Ho is in contact. Anything you or anyone else does will be at your own risk."

The other stared at him but hesitated. Et, still drunk on his own spurt of body adrenalin, pushed free of the security men, walked up to and past Rico and the man in black, and opened the door through which the other had come.

He stepped into what seemed to be a balcony with seats overlooking a gym. The seats were sparsely filled with spectators hunched over viewscreens that gave them a closeup of action on the gym floor. At one end of the gym some kind of tally board burned with lights. Down on the floor of the gym itself, two men in black suits like those on the men in the corridor were engaged in a fencing match.

It was all so commonplace and harmless that Et halted, ready to feel foolish at forcing his way in.

Then he noticed that neither of the fencers wore masks. Nor were they fitted with mesh shirts for electrical scoring of touches. Instead, they were naked to the waist; and the one on the right had a long red line slantwise across the upper left of his chest.

Et stepped forward to an empty seat and looked into the viewer before it.

The viewer gave him an excellent closeup. It was as if he looked at the fencers from less than six feet away. He saw then that the weapons had no protective buttons. Their points were sharp. As he looked, the arm of the man on the left straightened in a lunge and the point of his weapon disappeared into the already scratched chest of his adversary.

As the man on the right crumpled, Et turned dazedly and pushed his way back out the door. Rico and the security men were waiting for him.

"All right," said Et thickly. "We'll go."

Silently, they went, the black-clad men moving out of their way as they approached. Still in silence, Et rode the elevator to his own corridor and his own suite. He fell on his back on the bed, staring at the ceiling. The exhausted feeling was back. The headache was like a tourniquet about his temples. But more than that was churning inside him. He had seen fights, plenty of them. He had even seen knives and bottles and clubs used, and he was aware that waivers could be signed allowing two contestants to fence with naked weapons.

But the presence of the security men and the tote board confirmed that this had been something more, a cold-blooded duel to the death taking place only so that spectators could bet on it.

With that ugly image still floating in his mind, he fell into an uneasy sleep.

6

He dreamed that he was busy building something beautiful and intricate. In a very large room, he was constructing all sorts of different shapes out of small crystalline shapes. Pillars, arches, and fragile enclosures—they covered the available floor surface and stretched from floor to ceiling. The facets and angles of their innumerable tiny crystals reflected points of fire in all colors around him: diamond-white, red, green, purple, yellow. . . .

A hand blundered into the room, a massive chunk of flesh and bone cut off at the wrist, bigger than a man, bigger than Et. Blindly and brainlessly, it began to draw straight lines along the floor, arbitrarily dividing the room into sections. It followed the line it was drawing without regard for what was in the way, smashing through and destroying the crystalline creations in its path.

The room was being plowed into a shambles. Desperately, Et grappled with the hand, trying to stop it. But it was too massive for him to halt or push aside. With stupid but inexorable concentration it continued, leaving ruin and havoc behind it, all the bright firepoints of light extinguished forever, while Et struggled helplessly with it, in a vain effort to stop the destruction. . . .

He woke to find himself on the hotel bed in a darkened room, with a darker shape that resolved itself into Rico standing over him.

"What time is it?" said Et thickly.

"Nearly noon," said Rico, "local Hong Kong time."

"How long was I sleeping?"

"About four hours."

"Only four hours?" Et felt like a man in hell, exhausted and tense at the same time. His mouth and throat were dry as powder, his head beat with pain to the pulse of his heart, and all the muscles of his body felt as if he had just climbed a mountain.

"Only four hours. Mr. Ho," said Rico, "I suggest we go to your island now. Your doctor will be waiting for you there, a physician who specializes in the problems of R-Masters. You need his help."

"What help?" said Et, forcing himself up on his elbow. He peered up through the gloom at Rico. "No medicines. No drugs."

"You're not being realistic," Rico said. "The R-47 changes your whole physical system permanently. There are prescriptions to help you live with these changes—only they're necessarily different for each R-Master. Your physician will have to examine you and determine what you need."

"Nothing," said Et. With a sudden effort he got himself up in sitting condition on the side of the bed. "There's nothing I need. Yes—I need food. And coffee. Now! As quick as you can."

"Yes, Mr. Ho."

Rico went off. Et fumbled his way to a shower; the hot water helped to revive him. He shaved, found some clean clothes laid out on a chair, and put them on. By the time he was dressed, Rico had returned, with another man pushing a wheeled cart on which were covered plates. The good odor of coffee rose into Et's nostrils.

He drank and ate. Nothing tasted quite right. In spite of its enticing odor, the coffee was harsh and acid, while the omelet and toast that went with it were almost tasteless. But with food inside him he began to feel once more in control of his life.

He made himself drink more coffee.

"Rico," he said. "I want to talk to another R-Master. Will you set that up?"

For the first time since Et had met him, the secretary hesitated.

"I'll try, of course, Mr. Ho," he said. "But you understand—with other Masters we can only ask."

Et frowned.

"You mean out of sixty or whatever number there are of them, there wouldn't be one who could spare me an hour or two of talk?"

"They all have their own individual ways," said Rico. He turned to go, then looked back. "I assume you'd rather talk to a Master who was a man?"

Et blinked and grinned. He had not thought that far into the matter.

"You're right," he said. "In this one case, you're right. I'd rather talk to another R-Master who's a man."

Rico went out. Fifteen minutes later, he was back.

"Master Lee Malone will be glad to talk to you, his secretary says, Mr. Ho. I'm sorry."

"Sorry? Why?"

"Master Lee Malone is . . . a little eccentric, even for a Master," said Rico. "He's always willing to talk to new Masters, but I don't know how informative or useful he'll be. But there's no one else who wants to be disturbed among the others—men or women."

Et nodded. He was feeling better than he had for some time. The taste of the coffee had come back to naturalness with his third cup, and he sipped at the hot liquid now.

"All right," he said quietly. "I'm thankful to anyone who'll give me the time. I'll have my session with this Malone, and then we'll go to that island you want to get me to. But Rico—"

"Yes, sir?"

"No more talk about medicines or drugs for me."

"I won't mention it again," said the secretary.

"Good. Now," said Et, "where does Master Malone keep himself?"

"North America, in San Diego, California," said Rico. "The EC courier intercontinental that brought you here is standing by. We can use it until you reach the island and your own assigned craft."

"All right," said Et, getting up from his chair and his coffee cup. "We'll go right now."

R-Master Lee Malone did not merely live in San Diego, he lived in one of the old museum sections of San Diego. There were areas of the town that had been carefully preserved, and dated back to before the time when San Diego's residential streets went underground—twenty years before they were disposed of entirely. To get to Malone's residence, it was necessary to take an air taxi from the port to the edge of the museum area and then switch to one of the hovercars which were the only transportation allowed. They were once more on the night side of the planet, 10 P.M. of a chilly evening untypical of San Diego. Their hovercar followed programming faithfully through the cold, shallow, concrete troughs of the streets, under old-fashioned street lamps, past cement-block and wooden walls that had been erected during the riots of the last decade of the twentieth century, to hide and protect these one-family homes. At last it stopped before a modern metal vehicle door in a poured ceramic wall. Et got out, but Rico stayed where he was in the hovercar. Et looked at him questioningly.

"Master Malone specified he would see you only," said Rico.

Et nodded. He turned toward the vehicle door and saw that a personnel slot had now opened in it. He walked through, and the slot closed behind him.

He found himself in an area about four times the size of the individual lots he had seen pictured in history books. Under the illumination of some grav-float floodlights, he saw ahead of him a large rambling structure that seemed to be made of wood. Between this building and himself was an extensive grassy area thickly shadowed by large old trees; he recognized oak and what seemed to be cottonwood, among others. But the house was unkempt-appearing and badly in need of paint. The grass of the lawn stood high. Cardboard and wooden signs were inexpertly nailed or glued to the tree trunks, while various specimens of broken lawn furniture and other bits of household debris lay scattered about. The whole area had the look of the scene of a destructive lawn party that had not been cleaned up for veral years.

One of the shallow cement troughs, which had evidently been intended once as a driveway, led up to the house. Et walked up it, leaving it finally for the front door, a wide and tall surface of dark wood, across which had been clumsily painted in red letters MOGOW.

The word—if it was a word—rang a faint bell of familiarity. Et turned from the door to look back into the front yard. Several of the signs on the trees had the same combination of letters, either as part of a longer screed or by themselves. He turned back to the door and looked around for an annunciator plate. There was none visible. Remembering the room in which he had awakened on the morning after taking the R-47, he bent the knuckles of his right hand and rapped on the wood surface itself.

The door opened to reveal a short, thin, but broad-shouldered man with a wispy yellow beard and yellowish-gray hair.

"Come in! Come on, then!" he snapped in an old man's voice. "I'm Malone; you're Ho. Come in before I change my mind and kick you out, after all."

Et grinned.

"What's funny?" demanded Malone, as the door closed itself behind them.

"I was just thinking," Et said. "I haven't felt like any kind of a R-Master so far. And you certainly don't look or sound like one."

Malone looked at him. Suddenly the old face changed. The lines of irascibility smoothed out, the down-curving line of the old lips became level, and the eyes darkened, hooded under the tangled gray brows.

"Don't be a damn fool," said Malone quietly, in a younger voice. "Keep your mouth shut until you know what you're talking about."

He turned and led the way through a series of dark rooms and hallways and at last through a door that let them into a room miserly of window space but rich in interior decoration and a warmly lighted fireplace. The furniture was heavy, ancient, and comfortably over-stuffed; the rugs were thick and dark-colored.

"Sit down," said Malone, throwing himself into one of a pair of high-backed chairs flanking the fireplace. "I suppose you found out I was the only one of us who'd talk to you."

"That's right," said Et.

"Of course it's right," said Malone. His voice was back on its cracking, irascible old-man's note. "But don't blame them. In fact, make a good start of it. Don't *blame* anyone —except yourself. No one twisted your arm to make you take the R-47. So forget about blaming and concentrate on what can be done; that's my advice."

He looked into the dancing flames.

"Not that you'll take it—probably," he said.

"Why shouldn't I?" Et asked. "It makes sense."

Malone looked up from the fire at him and their gazes locked.

"People seem to run on rails, no matter what I tell them," said the older man softly. "Take you, now. So far you've done everything wrong, every time you had a choice. To begin with, what status did you opt for with the EC, Ward or Citizen? No, don't tell me. I'll tell you. You picked citizen status, didn't you?"

"I shouldn't have?"

"Hell, no!" snapped Malone. "Couldn't you see that choice was being forced on you?"

"I've got things I want to do," said Et. "I needed the extra freedom."

"*Extra* freedom!" Malone snorted. "The only status that gives you anything approaching some freedom is Ward. What do you think I am?"

"Ward, obviously," said Et.

"That's right. But then I was one of the early ones. Know how long I've been a Master?"

Et shook his head.

"Forty years."

Et looked at him closely. It was not that Malone looked hardly more than his late fifties, until he spoke. There were ninety- and hundred-year-olds around nowadays who could pass for Malone's younger brother. It was the fact that if Malone was telling the truth he must have been among the first half dozen or so of the Masters to be produced by R-47.

"That's right, forty years," said Malone. "And I'm the only Master left that goes anywhere near that far back. But you won't listen to me, any more than any of the others I've talked to ever did."

"You keep insisting on that," said Et gently, "and maybe you'll end up talking me into it."

Malone stared at him for a second and then burst into a shout of laughter, not an aged cackle, but a full-throated roar of humor.

"All right!" he said. "All right! Maybe you're worth the trouble, after all. But let's look at what you've done so far."

"I—" began Et, but Malone cut him short.

"Don't tell me! I'll tell you," he said. "I have myself briefed on what every new Master does, as soon as he reacts to the R-47. Not that I need briefing any more. I know without being told what you or anyone else is going to do first—and it's always the wrong things. Take you. First you tried to see how much the EC would do for you. Then you tried to see how much they'd spend on you. Then, when you got nowhere with both tries, you finally thought of doing what you should have thought of in the first place—asking somebody who knows. But nobody who knows would talk to you but me. And the way things are set up I don't look like anyone you can trust, even if I do tell you."

"Look," said Et. He had liked the other man without reason, from the first moment of seeing him. But he was heavy with tiredness and his head throbbed. "Just answer a few questions. Why don't I feel like I'm an R-Master, if I am one?"

"Why, now," said Malone, "don't tell me you feel just like you always did?"

"Of course I—" Et broke off. "You mean the way I feel now? I'm out on my feet and uncomfortable right now. But don't tell me . . ."

He paused.

"Or," he went on slowly, "do tell me, come to think of it. Do you mean anyone who has the kind of reaction to R-47 that makes him an R-Master is bound to go around feeling this bad? You mean all sixty-three Masters feel like this all the time?"

Malone chuckled.

"I don't," he answered, "but I'm different. The rest—yes, they feel like you do, most of the time. The only time they don't is when they get worked up about something, worked up enough to override their ordinary sensations with excitement, such as when they're figuring something out, or when they're doped up with medicines that damp out their discomforts."

He laughed sarcastically.

"Shakes you up, doesn't it?" he said. "You thought being a lucky ticket holder in the Reninase-47 sweepstakes was nothing but peaches and cream. Why should it be? Your whole system's been kicked out of focus to gear up along with a mind that's now overgeared. Ever hear of medicines with side effects? Hell, they've all got side effects, even the ones where you don't feel the effects consciously! The history of medicine is lousy with side effects, loaded with drugs that would have been perfect in their main effect if there just hadn't been a few kicker results there, too, that might kill the patient or make him wish he'd never been born. All right, R-47 makes men or women into R-Masters, all right, in a few stray cases. But when it does, the heavy effect it has on intelligence is matched by just as heavy effects on the rest of the person it works on."

Et nodded. "I see," he said.

"Come on now," said Malone. "Don't just sit there and pretend to shrug it off. Wait until the chemicals in you wear off—whatever drugs your EC doctor first pumped into you—if you think you feel bad now!"

"What drugs? When?" Et demanded.

"How do I know what drugs? I wasn't there when you had your first R-47 reaction!" Malone snapped. "As for when, you know that better than I do. When did you last see the physician EC assigned you?"

"I haven't seen him at all yet," said Et. "And when and if I do, he can keep any medicines he's got on hand. I don't take them."

You don't mean you haven't had anything but the initial R-47 injection?"

"Not unless they pumped something into me while I was asleep or unconscious."

Malone leaned forward in his chair and peered into Et's eyes with a suddenly sharp gaze.

"You sure you're telling me the truth?" he demanded. "How do you feel?"

"I don't feel good," said Et grimly. "But I'm alive and moving, and I plan to keep on moving."

"Hmmm," said Malone thoughtfully. "Either you've got some sort of lucky easy reaction to the side effects of R-47 or you're tougher than bull leather. And you never take medicines—any medicines?"

"Not since I could walk."

"How about aspirin?"

"No."

"Tobacco? Alcohol? Cannabis?"

"No tobacco. No cannabis. Alcohol, yes," said Et. "I used to be able to drink and never have a hangover." He grimaced. "I can't now; you're right about the side effects as far as that goes. I get hangovers."

"Coffee?"

"Coffee's fine. I've even drunk some since the R-47. Tastes a little bad sometimes. But the effect seems good enough."

"Tea? Maté?"

"I didn't use to drink tea much. Haven't tried it since the R-47. Maté I never did drink."

"Cough syrup? Codeine?"

"I wouldn't touch it. Not that I ever had a lot of coughs. Nor did I ever use breath mints, laxatives, antihistamines—"

"You'd better keep some antihistamines around, at any rate," said Malone dryly. "You may find you've become allergy-prone. Something like a bee sting can always happen, and anaphylactic shock can kill you in minutes."

"I'll take my chances," said Et.

Malone shook his head slowly.

"You're something different," he said, "unless I'm mistaken—and I'm not mistaken about most things. Tell me something. What if you have to give up alcohol and coffee too. Will you suffer?"

"I've just about decided to give up alcohol, and I'd miss coffee," said Et. "But understand me. Any time I have to, I can give up anything but water, food, and breathing—and under the proper conditions I'd be willing to give even those a try."

"Tell me about yourself," said Malone.

Et did. Starting with his Polynesian childhood, up through his years of education, to the years sailing the *Sarah* and further to the death of Wally and his own decision to take the R-47.

"All right," said Malone at last. He sat back in his chair. The moving firelight left shadows in the lines of his face that made those lines seem deeper and older. "Now *I'll* tell you a story. The world's going to hell in a handbasket —yes, you heard me right. To hell in a handbasket, in spite of all the peace and prosperity and Citizen's Basic Allowances, and all the services. Can you believe that?"

"I can," said Et. "Should I, though?"

"Make up your own mind. I'm just telling a story. Here's this world, going to hell, and a man like yourself hits on a long chance that lands him right in the middle of the machinery causing all the trouble."

Et felt a surge of alertness through him that signaled the same sort of body adrenalin reaction he had had in the Sunset Hut.

"Go on," he said. "What machinery? What trouble?"

"You're an R-Master," said Malone, almost evilly. "Figure it out."

"But am I?" Et asked. "That was one of the questions I asked you. If I've got all this extra intelligence, why don't I feel it?"

"Who says you've got something you can 'feel'?" said Malone. "Was there ever a time you were able to 'feel' how bright you were? Of course not. The only way you ever knew you had any brains was when you noticed the people around doing something to show they didn't have as many as you."

Malone snorted. "You offered to work for the EC," he went on. "Wait about six months or so, until their people come to you with a problem and you take a look at it and see there's no real problem there. Any idiot, you realize, could fix their trouble. But you tell them what to do anyway, and they thank you and go away. You'll wonder if they were just pretending to have a problem, because certainly anyone ought to see what you saw. Then maybe—just maybe—you'll begin to understand the gap between you and other people and see what they mean by 'R-Master.' But even then, *even then,* you won't 'feel' any different from the way you felt since you first opened your eyes on this world."

He stopped.

"On the other hand, in these side effects," he added, "you've got a whole fistful of feelings—if body sensations are what you want."

"If there's something extra there in the intelligence area, I ought to be able to sense it," said Et stubbornly.

"Who says it has to be something extra?" growled Malone. "Nobody understands what R-47 does. They think it's only an irritant, a superpep pill that makes your thinking machinery whir twice as fast as it's designed to whir. R-Masters don't live long, generally; they average about ten years or so after they've taken the R-47."

"How about you?" said Et.

"I told you I was different."

"Why are you?"

"Who knows?" snarled Malone. "If anyone had the answer to that, I would, being the man concerned and having a Master's mind to figure things out with. I don't know why I'm different. I am, though. For one thing, I've been a Master forty years and I've never needed their medicines. You understand? I didn't just tough it out, the way you're doing; I never felt bad at all."

"All right," said Et. "What's your advice for me? What should I do?"

"Why should I give you any advice?" snapped Malone.

A surge of adrenalin cleared Et's head for a moment. "Well, I'll tell you," he said, quietly and slowly. "You struck me as a fairly reasonable sort the moment you opened the door. Now if you'd asked me for advice, I probably would have given it to you, just for the reason that there doesn't seem any reason not to. It seems to me you've got as little reason not to help me as I'd have had not to help you."

Malone snorted. But the snort died and there was a moment of silence.

"All right," he said, after that moment. "I'll tell you

what I'll do. See if you can last a year of it—with this business of yours of not letting them help you with medicines. Then, if you haven't figured it all out yourself by that time, come back here and I'll tell you anything I know. And that's that! End of interview!"

"If that's the best you can do," said Et.

He got to his feet. Malone also stood up and led the way back out the way they had come in. Malone himself opened the front door—Et had seen no sign to indicate that even one other person shared the house with the other man—and Et stepped back out onto the front steps.

He turned as the door was about to close behind him.

"What does MOGOW mean?" he asked.

Malone almost glared at him.

"What you were one of once yourself," he said, back again into the high voice of age, "whether you knew it or not. Men of Good Will!"

He slammed the door shut. Et turned and walked back down the long drive, past the unmowed grass, the litter of signs on the trees. The personnel slot on the door was open, and he went through it to find the hovercar with Erm still waiting for him.

"To the island, Mr. Ho?" Rico said, as the car started up.

Et nodded. Now that it was all over, he was too exhausted to talk. He closed his eyes. Against the darkness of the inner lids, enormous, glowing letters danced crazily: MEN OF GOOD WILL.

7

The trip back to the intercontinental and the ride across to the Caribbean passed in a daze for Et. He roused only when he had to move from vehicle to vehicle. Finally, when the island was reached, he was conscious of stumbling along under a sky that was still night-dark, but now warm. From the pad on which the intercontinental had landed, Rico and one of the security guards took him up a ramp to a slidewalk, which happily took over the effort of transporting him toward a series of interconnected buildings.

The slidewalks carried them eventually through the entrance of one of the buildings into simulated daylight and a small crowd of waiting people. Among them was Carwell, standing—looming—beside a shorter man with jet-black hair and a bushy black brush of a mustache that gave him an irritable look. But Carwell and the other man, as well as all but one of the others waiting, evaporated almost immediately from Et's consciousness. The one who remained was Alaric.

"Al!" croaked Et. "Al, come on with me."

Alaric, who had been standing back in the crowd, pushed past other bodies and joined Et on the still-moving slideway.

"Stick with me, Al," said Et. "I'm making you my chief of security."

Al nodded.

The slidewalk carried them on. They transferred to another moving walkway and ended at last before a door that slid aside to let them into a wide bedroom, which at first seemed open to the tropic night, until a glint of reflected light from the wall illumination panels showed Et that a transparent roof was overhead. He was helped to an enormous, floating grav bed and dropped onto it.

"Al!" he called.

Al loomed up at the side of the bed, pushing his way between Carwell and the man with the black mustache.

"There you are," said Et, with effort. "Carwell, no one's to touch me. You know what I told you about drugs. Al, you're in charge. Get everyone but yourself out of here. I need sleep."

"Mr. Ho," broke in the man with the mustache. "I'm Dr. Hoskides, your physician, assigned by the EC. I won't be responsible—"

"Then don't be. I relieve you of responsibility. Out," said Et. "Carwell, Rico—everybody out."

"Etter—" began Carwell.

"Out. Get them out, Al."

The faces began to move back from the side of his bed, to vanish from the blurred circle of his vision. He looked at the thickly strewn stars above him and then forced his eyelids closed. It was like trying to go to sleep on a not stove, but he made an image in his mind of a house in the midst of a battle, a house with one secret room. And in that secret room he locked himself, lay down, reached out to the light controls, and turned them downward. Gradually the one illumination panel in the secret room dimmed, and dimmed, and went out. . . .

At intervals after that he drifted back to wakening again and then forced himself back down under the locks and bolts of sleep.

Finally he came awake beyond all denying, although he lay still for a long time, with his eyes stubbornly closed, trying to hold on to slumber. At last he gave up and opened his eyes. Around him the room was empty, the ceiling overhead was opaqued to a night dimness, and a barely visible Al sat in a tall-backed grav float beside the door.

"Al?" said Et.

The small man got up from his float, walked to the bed, and stood looking down at him.

"How do you feel?" asked Alaric.

Et grimaced. He had forgotten how he felt, but now he remembered.

"Not good," he said. "I've got a sour taste in my mouth, a headache, and a backache. I feel starved to death and a little sick at my stomach at the same time. But I got some sleep; my head's clear."

"All right," said Al. "That's all right, then."

"You kept everybody out?"

Al nodded.

"They only tried to come in once or twice. I told them not to push it, and they didn't." Al looked down at Et. "You slept hard. Most of the time you looked dead. I had to take your pulse a couple of times to be sure you were still alive. Every so often, though, you thrashed around like you were fighting sharks."

"Maybe I was," said Et. He could not remember specific dreams, but in the back of his mind there was the feeling of nightmares. "But it was worth it. As I say, my mind's clear now. I can think."

Al still stood looking down at him.

"You don't act much different," he said.

"I don't feel different," Et said. "I don't know—there's more to this whole business than I ever imagined."

"Why did you go take the R-47, anyway?" said Al. "Hell, you hardly saw that brother of yours twice a year before he took it."

"I know," said Et. "That was one of the reasons."

"Anyway," said Al. "There's a reason I wanted to see you once more anyway. To see what it'd done to you. Now I do see. It's geared up that old responsibility side of you."

"Old responsibility side?" Et stared at the smaller man. "What old responsibility side?"

"The one you always had," Al said. "For everything. Women, stray dogs and cats—me, even."

Et took a deep breath and lay looking at the ceiling.

"I learn something every day," he said.

"You didn't know it showed?" Al said. "You ought to have known."

"I didn't know, period," said Et. "Never mind. I suppose I'd better eat something. Food and sleep, that's what I have to run on, and I've had the sleep."

"I'll get it for you," Al said. "What do you want?"

"Anything," said Et, and grimaced again. "I'm hollow, but nothing I think of seems as if it would taste good. Get me a steak and some orange juice. A lot of orange juice."

"Right," said Al. He went toward the door. "Shall I let

any of them in? They all want in to see you."

"After I've eaten. Then—only Carwell," said Et.

Al went out. Et lay back, thinking. As he had said to Al, his mind was clear now. It worked. Whether it was working with some sort of superspeed or supercapacity there was no way of knowing, but it occurred to him that he had deduced a great deal—a very great deal—in the last day or two, about life and the world. For twenty-four years he had gone on certain assumptions; now, in three days, he had been forced to discover that most of those assumptions either contained errors or were downright false. If they were false, the world itself could be something he had never guessed. And Wally's part in it could be something he had not understood at all.

He had no definite proof of any of this yet. He had no specifics. But the conviction in him was becoming overwhelming that he had somehow been dealing with the misleading surface of a world, bearing no relation to the reality underneath it.

The steak and orange juice were brought in by Al and proved at least partly a disappointment. The steak was as tasteless as the breakfast he had last eaten had been. The orange juice, on the other hand, seemed disagreeably acid. Nonetheless, the food and drink, once it was down, conquered the slight nausea he had been feeling and made him feel nourished.

"I'll see Carwell now," he told Al.

Carwell came in, looking apologetic and stern at the same time. Et was lying on his bed surface once more, and Carwell seated his large bulk on a grav float at the edge of the bed.

"How are you feeling?" Carwell asked.

"Uncomfortable—but awake and fed," said Et. "I gather you decided to take me up on my offer to take care of me?"

"Yes," Carwell said. "But I don't know how I or anyone else can do much for you medically if you won't take advice. Officially—if I am your physician officially—I have to protest the fact that you won't let Dr. Hoskides near you."

"Hoskides is the man with the mustache, my EC doctor?"

"That's right," said Carwell, "and an extremely competent physician, as well as being a specialist in your type of case—which I'm not."

"What is this?" Et asked. "The EC speaking even through you?"

"My ethics as a doctor speaking," said Carwell. "I'm willing to be your physician; truthfully, it's a job that intrigues me. But I have to tell you honestly that I think Dr. Hoskides is much better able to take care of you than I am."

"All right," said Et. "You've officially protested, and I've officially listened to your protest and filed it. Now, Dr. Hoskides can do anything he wants. I'll be glad to have him stay around, and you two can talk together, consult or whatever, about me as much as you like. But as far as I'm concerned, I deal with you and you only. Is that situation going to work with you, or is it impossible?"

"It's going to have to work," said Carwell. "There's no way we can bring pressure on you. Even if you weren't an R-Master, you've got the right of every competent human being on Earth to choose his own physician and medical care."

"Good," said Et. "Now that that's settled, would you check me over and tell me what you think?"

Carwell did.

"As far as I can tell," he said at the end of about ten minutes, "you're normally healthy. Your pulse is a little fast, but your blood pressure is low normal. You seem to be somewhat more tense than when I first checked you out before the R-47 injection. What do you feel?"

"Generally hangoverish," said Et. "Slight headache, backache, heavy-bodied. . . ." He ran through a list of minor symptoms.

Carwell shook his head.

"Are those standard reactions for an R-Master?" Et asked.

"There is no standard, evidently, from what I can learn," Carwell said. "It's different for each Master; all each assigned physician does is try to give his patient as much symptomatic relief as possible without causing him other discomforts."

"I see," said Et. "You know, there's an interesting point in connection with that. It occurs to me that the one thing I haven't got so far has been information."

"What do you want to know?" asked Carwell.

"In your department," said Et, "everything that's known about R-47, its development, its effects on people: how many people take it, what the true percentage of idiots and Masters produced is—everything. How do you like the idea of being a researcher?"

"Everybody who goes into medicine thinks about doing research at one time or another," said Carwell. "I've had my own dreams, too. You want me to look into that?"

"Yes. Tell whoever you have to that you're doing it for me, but don't tell them why."

"I don't know why," said Carwell.

"You don't—" Et caught himself up short. "Of course

you don't. That's right. Well, go ahead; and remember, while you're at it, keep what's-his-name, Hoskides, away from me."

"I'll certainly try," said Carwell. He went out.

Et lay for a second, watching the closed door through which Carwell had just passed.

"Al," he said.

Al came up to the side of the bed.

"You said something about seeing me once more," Et told him. "You weren't planning to turn around and leave me here?"

"You won't want somebody like me around now," said Al.

"Why not?"

Al looked down at him strangely.

"All right," Al said, "maybe I wouldn't want to be around someone who knows I'm that much dumber than he is."

"You'll only be dumber than I am if you make yourself out that way," said Et. "Al, nothing about this R-Master business is the way people—people like us—used to think it was. It may not be a matter of intelligence at all."

"I don't get you," said Al.

"I don't get me, either," said Et. "I'm crocked-up from the side effects of this R-47, and to top it off all of a sudden the world seems to be ninety degrees turned from what I thought it was. All I know is I need help. I need someone to back me I can trust. If you go, who've I got?"

Al frowned.

"You always had an edge," he said. "You don't have to be an R-Master now to talk me into something."

"Will you hang around awhile and then make up your mind about staying?"

"Yes," said Al, after a second. "I can do that, all right."

"Thanks," said Et. "I mean that. I—oh, hell!"

"What?"

Et laughed.

"I wanted you to have the *Sarah*," he said. "But if I offer her to you now, it'll sound like I'm trying to pay you for staying."

"That's all right," said Al. "I'll take the *Sarah* under any conditions, any time. She's nothing to you, now, but she's still a lot to me."

Et shook his head.

"I'm glad you'll take her," he said. "But I haven't changed that much. That's one of the things I hope you'll find out. Anyway—who's waiting to see me, if anyone?"

"Mainly that Rico Erm."

"Good. Come to think of it," said Et, "there's something I want him to check up on for me. Let him in next."

Al opened the door and, putting his head through the opening, said something Et could not catch. Then the smaller man stood back, and Rico walked in. Ignoring Al, he came directly to Et.

"Mr. Ho," he said, "there's a large staff involved in running this island. I have to know what you want, so I can give them their orders."

"I want absolute privacy, unless I say otherwise," said Et. "Especially, I don't want the security men to follow me around. By the way, Alaric Amundssen, here, is to be put on the payroll—I assume there's a payroll?"

Rico nodded.

"I also want him officially named head of my security staff."

"Mr. Ho, I can't promise that. The Security Division comes from the Auditor Corps, and they go to a great deal of trouble to train and educate their workers."

"Ask them if they'd like me to shut them out completely the way I'm shutting out Dr. Hoskides. Come to think of it, I want Carwell appointed my personal physician and put on the payroll too."

"I'll put the request in, Mr. Ho. Now—"

"I'm not through," Et said. "I want the most complete library unit made available to me—"

"We already have one here."

"Good. And from time to time I'm going to want to talk to experts in various fields. One more thing. I said that I wanted to talk to a Miss Maea Tornoy, a temporal sociologist—"

"She's already here."

"Send her in, then. No"—Et made an effort and sat up on the edge of the bed, made a further effort and stood up —"wait a minute, I'd better get dressed first."

"I'll send her to you when you're ready, Mr. Ho," said Rico. "You'll find clothes that fit you in the closet there. May I ask one thing, though? Are you planning on leaving this island again in the next twenty-four hours?"

"I don't think so."

"Thank you. Then I can order the staff accordingly. Good morning." Rico turned toward the door, and this time he crossed gazes with Alaric. "Good morning, Mr. Amundssen."

"Al," said Al.

"Good morning, Al."

"Morning," said Al as Rico went out of the room, shutting the door behind him. He watched the door close before turning back to Et. "Actually, it's just about noon."

"Time to move," said Et, going to the closet and opening it. "I'll get dressed. Have you been around the island? Where's a good place to sit down and talk with a girl?"

"There's a terrace looking down a slope to the boat dock," said Al. "I'll show you."

Fifteen minutes later, sitting on a white-painted wrought-iron chair on the flagstone terrace, overlooking a low flagstone wall and a lawn falling away to what was more like a small marina than a simple dock, Et glanced up to see Al bringing in Maea Tornoy. He stood up.

"Et," she said, as they faced each other at last. "It's so good to see you again. I didn't know about Wally until just last week. Was there a funeral?"

"No," said Et. "They put him in cryogenic automatically. I've been told there's no point in trying revival. But we're going to try anyway."

"I'm so sorry."

"Yes." Et did not want to discuss Wally directly with her. Everything that had happened since had driven the matter about her and Wally into the back of his mind, but seeing her reminded him of it again.

After the startling loveliness of Cele Partner Maea's appearance was not breathtaking—but then, someone like Cele was almost unreal. In her own fashion, Maea had beauty enough. Her hair was long and auburn, shading to red. She was relatively tall, like Cele, but more strongly boned, so that she moved with the odd sort of angular grace seen sometimes in adolescent girls or in very athletic women. In a peculiar way, she was more female and real than Cele, who had a touch of the occult about her, like a figure that had stepped out of a painting.

"Maybe we can talk about Wally a little later," said Et as they sat down. "Right now, I'm too wound up in adjusting to being an R-Master. If you can help me with that first, I'd appreciate it."

"Of course," she said. "What can I do?"

"Tell me something about what your specialty covers," he said. "I know temporal sociology deals with the development and change in human institutions. But you specialize in making forecasts, don't you, of the changes that'll take place if a community, or a city, puts a particular alteration or development into effect?"

"That's my particular specialty," Maea said. "A temporal psychologist can be involved in any aspect of changing human conditions. It's like being a psychologist; the name covers so many specialties it doesn't mean anything by itself. Like saying someone's an engineer. Unless you specify what kind of engineer, she or he could be anything."

"All right," said Et. "What I want from you is a quick survey, or directions from you on how to make a quick survey, of changes since R-47 was first invented."

"It wasn't invented. It was an accidental discovery. Like penicillin."

"Whatever," said Et.

"There's no problem in that," Maea said. "Your secretary says you've got a full-scale library machine here. I can program a course of references for you that will give you a running picture of change from any time to the present. But you'll have to tell me what you're after. General technological development? Development of human emotional patterns? Political developments?"

"I want to know," said Et, "how much influence R-47, in both its failures and its successes, like me, has had on the general direction society has taken since, say, the year 2000."

"All right. Next question. How extensive a survey do you want to make? I mean, how much studying do you want to do?"

"Give me something I can go through in a day or so, say the equivalent of four or five ordinary-size book-length references."

"All right." She looked at him keenly and a little questioningly. Her face was rounded, and a light dusting of freckles showed across her nose like ghosts of childhood under the golden tan of her skin. "I'll get busy, then."

She stood up. He stood up with her.

"As soon as I've had a chance to go through the references, we'll talk some more," he said. "I didn't pull you away from some particularly important job to get you here, did I? I'm sorry if I did."

"No," she said. "As it happened, I was between jobs."

She turned and went off, through the door from the terrace back into the house, drawing his gaze after her.

Et turned back to the lawn and sat down again. During his talk with Maea the adrenalin surge had begun in him, and he felt almost normal. He reached out to the little table beside his chair and pressed the phone stud.

"Rico?" he said.

There was a moment's pause; then Rico's voice answered.

"Yes, Mr. Ho."

"Bring out a terminal to that library machine, will you? I might as well work here as any place else. Oh, and see if you can find Dr. Carwell and have him step out here and speak to me for a moment."

"Yes, Mr. Ho."

A few minutes later Rico showed up, followed by a man pushing a reading screen library terminal along on a table-height grav float. They left, and a few minutes later Morgan Carwell appeared.

"Just a quick question or two," Et said to the big physician. "How did I act while I was unconscious—I mean, between the time I collapsed as I was leaving the clinic and when I woke up in that bedroom with the old-fashioned furniture?"

"I wasn't with you," said Carwell. "Our clinic chief—you met Dr. Lopayo, didn't you?—took care of you during those hours. I assumed from what he said that you had the normal reaction."

"What's the normal reaction?"

"Why, simply a quiet period of nonconsciousness while the shock of the mental change is absorbed—according to the books."

"Check up," said Et. "Find out if I did go according to the books. And," he said as Carwell turned away, "one other thing. Will you program a short study course for me in R-47, its discovery, its history, and everything else about it?"

"If you like," said Carwell. "But Dr. Hoskides is much more qualified—"

"Dr. Hoskides is to have nothing to do with this—or with me. Now or in the future," said Et.

"Very well," said Carwell, shrugging. He went off, and Et turned to the library terminal, typing out his request.

MEN OF GOOD WILL, so-called. Or MOGOW. Any reference or other information under these cues.

Heat—a warmth like that of a fever—was beginning to glow all through him. He felt his thoughts picking up speed under the powerful thrust of the R-47–induced stimulation. A problem lay before him now, and he hurled himself with increasing speed to engage it, like a lover to a tryst or a warrior to a battle.

8

Three days later he called a meeting on the terrace. Seated around him were Alaric, Carwell, and Maea. Standing—having politely declined to sit—was Rico.

"All right," said Et grimly, looking around at all of them. "it's the witching hour. Time to take off our masks."

They all gazed back at him. It was Maea who spoke first.

"Masks?" she said. "What masks?"

"Everyone here except Al," said Et, "is wearing some kind of mask. Mine's the mask of a R-Master, for the moment. For the rest of you—Maea, you're a Woman of Good Will. There's an organization called Men of Good Will, and you belong to it."

He turned to Carwell.

"You too," he said. "You're a Man of Good Will—though I don't know if you knew Maea was a fellow member."

"I didn't," said Carwell, staring across at her.

"Rico," said Et, looking at the secretary, "you're either

a spy deliberately attached to me by the Earth Council or a Man of Good Will yourself. Being what you are, you ought to be a spy. Doing what you've done since I've known you, you ought to be a member of the same loose organization as Maea and Morgan here. Which are you?"

Rico looked back at him calmly.

"If I may sit down, after all?" he said.

"Sit, stand, anything you like," said Et.

"Thank you," Rico stepped forward and seated himself on the extra grav-float seat that Et had provided for him originally. Seated, he seemed to change. It was a curious change, because there was no single specific sign of it in his face or body. But in some fashion he stopped being obliging and became almost commanding. "As a matter of fact, I'm neither."

"Then you'd better explain what you're doing being my secretary," said Et.

"I'll be glad to," said Rico. "And maybe you'll tell me how you discovered Maea Tornoy and Morgan Carwell belonged to the Men of Good Will. I wasn't aware of that myself. Which means the EC hadn't identified them as such, or I would have been notified that Security here on the island was to keep them under watch while they were here."

"In the case of Maea," said Et. "I found out her type of work had to bring her up against a situation existing on Earth right now, the same situation which has brought the Men of Good Will into existence. She'd have had either to ignore them or to join them, and the way the work she's done the past few years has been directed makes me believe she joined them. Morgan, here, struck me as preferring his work at the R-47 clinic to anything else. But when I asked him to give it up and become my personal doctor, he asked for time to think it over. Then, later, he accepted—still with no reason showing as to why he should leave the job he preferred."

Et broke off and looked hard at Carwell.

"I think he asked for time so that he could check with his own local branch of the Men of Good Will and then took their advice to accept the post because it might put him in a position to do something useful for the organization."

Carwell did not exactly blush; maturity and solidity had put him beyond blushing. But his embarrassed acknowledgment was marked as plainly on him as if it had been written on a card hung around his neck.

"Now what?" asked Maea.

"Now we consider Rico," said Et, turning back to the secretary, "who needs to declare himself."

"I've already declared myself," Rico answered. "The word I used was *neither*—neither spy nor Man of Good Will. I assigned myself to you, Etter Ho, on the basis of what you betrayed about yourself during a period of interrogation which took place between the time you collapsed at the clinic and when you woke up later."

"Al," said Et.

Al got up and slipped behind the float on which Rico was sitting.

"Don't be foolish," Rico said, without turning his head. "If I wanted to leave here none of you could stop me."

"Al might surprise you," said Et.

"I might have a few surprises to offer, myself," murmured Rico. "But all that's beside the point. You're concerned now, because your suspicion that something happened during your unconsciousness at the clinic has been confirmed, and by my use of the word 'interrogation.' But there's no reason for concern. It's standard EC practice to take advantage of the period of collapse following the making of an R-Master to compile a full dossier on him or her, using electropoint blockage of the brain's higher centers of restraint against cooperation."

"Where's the record of this interrogation of Et?" broke in Maea sharply.

Rico shrugged.

"The EC keeps such records in some safe place," he said. "But let me get to my point. I only had a second or two to glance over the dossier, but I was impressed by your deep sense of purpose against coercion, whether offered in the form of drugs or of controls imposed by society. I'm a perfectionist in all things myself, but I'd never before considered the possibilities of an individualist carrying his individualism to a state of perfection. I have enough seniority among the secretaries trained to work with R-Masters to pick my own assignment. So I picked you, and that's why I'm here."

"And now Et's going to get rid of you," said Al behind the float.

"That would be foolish," said Rico. "I have no special loyalty to the EC or to anyone or anything but my work. And I can be more useful than any of you dream."

"You think pretty well of yourself," said Maea.

"I should," said Rico. "I may not have quite the intellectual ability of an R-Master but I'm not far below that level, and that without ever coming close to R-47. I speak twenty-two languages and I have an eidetic memory. I actually hold two degrees in science and one in art, but I could easily hold a couple of dozen in either area. I was a Special Manager—an executive troubleshooter—for the EC for several years. I would be dropped into any situation or organization which wasn't performing as it should; it was my job to straighten things out within weeks. But after some years of this I began to see that a higher art than managing organizations was managing individuals, and I applied for a transfer to the occupation of R-Master's secretary. It's been a much more rewarding work. But it occurs to me now that there's one work higher yet, and that's to manage an idea, a purpose. I have no idea or purpose of my own, so I want to work with yours, Etter Ho."

Maea's gaze turned narrowly back on Et. "Purpose?" she asked.

Et sighed heavily.

"You people think in terms of capital letters, don't you?" he answered. "Yes, I've got a purpose. Not necessarily with a large P at the front of the word. I used to sail around the world not worrying about anything. Now I'm involved in what goes on in the world whether I want to be or not. If it was me, alone, I'd have nothing to do with Mogows or anything else. But I'm planning to bring Wally back, and my purpose is to keep both of us safe and untouched by the rest of the world. When he was alive, Wally was a Mogow, wasn't he?"

Et turned to look deliberately at Maea.

"Wasn't he?" Et repeated.

"Yes," said Maea calmly. "I suppose he told you about it?"

"No," said Et. "I didn't even know Mogows existed until I got hauled back into society by this R-47 reaction. But everything you people say is what I used to hear from Wally himself ever since we were boys. If he was a Mogow once, that's not too bad. I ought to be able to keep him from being one again. But meanwhile, a Mogow is one thing, a Mogow with a brother who's an R-Master, another. I want some sort of leverage with the Earth Council that'll make them believe me when I say Wally and I just want to be left alone."

"I doubt," said Rico in his precise voice, "that the EC would be seriously concerned by anything short of an R-Master who was himself a Mogow—an active Mogow, not just a talking one like R-Master Lee Malone. Generally speaking, the EC in my experience considers this gathering of idealists to be numerous but harmless, a loose, essentially unorganized movement. Consider the fact that the branch of the organization to which Morgan belongs clearly doesn't know what's being done by the organization to which Maea belongs. This shows how ineffective they are."

"It's just not practical to build a tight worldwide organization today in opposition to the established order," protested Carwell. "The practical difficulties are too great. Nowadays, no one can move around without leaving all sorts of evidence of where he's been—records of credit payments and the use of public equipment, like automated vehicles, lodging places, and stores."

"It's true," said Maea. "Each local organization of the Mogows has to operate pretty much on its own initiative. We just happen to live at a time when social and technological conditions are against us. It's a fact of life."

"It's a fact of intent," said Et bluntly. "Do you think it's sheer accident that for nearly forty years the mechanisms of society's control of the individual have developed and proliferated while the mechanisms that would protect the individual are inadequate?"

Maea and Carwell both stared at him.

"You mean the EC has deliberately. . . ? Oh, no," said Maea. "That's impossible. Government today is an open book. It hasn't any secrets for the same reason we individuals don't have privacy and freedom."

"God help us," said Et. "Rico, tell these fuzzy-minded idealists what their real enemy is."

"Certainly," said Rico. "It's a bureaucracy. *The* bureaucracy of the Earth Council. Not the individuals in that bureaucracy, though you'd have to give the ones in office at any time their share of guilt, but the bureaucratic system itself."

"But the failings of any bureaucratic system merely reflect the lack of good will among its workers . . ." Carwell began, and then trailed off.

"Forget your rhetoric," said Rico. "Look at the simple facts. Just one organization—the bureaucracy that's grown up around the Earth Council and its hundreds of subsidiary organizations and services—puts the food before every human on this planet daily and ensures the roof over his head every night. To be able to do that means to have the machinery of control, and the bureaucracy of the EC has got it."

"But you can't do away with that kind of human service," said Carwell. "I mean, somebody's got to do those jobs. All that's necessary is to make those doing it ethically and morally responsible, so that they won't take advantage of their power."

"Nonsense, doctor," said Rico. "You're missing the point. An ethical man survives in a bureaucratic post only if he puts his ethics in second place. A bureaucracy is like a living creature, with instincts of self-preservation and an urge to control all things for its own protection. The bureaucracy of the old Roman Empire didn't die when the Roman Empire died, it went on to flourish again in the bureaucracy of the medieval Catholic Christian Church. In just fifty years, thanks to a tremendously improved technology of communications and construction, they created a bureaucracy many times greater than anything dreamed of during the old Roman Empire. And this new bureaucracy of ours wants to continue to exist, whether individual humans or human institutions survive its controls or not."

Carwell shook his head, opened his mouth as if to argue, and closed it again on silence. He looked appealingly across at Maea.

"No," said Maea. "They're right. I began to run into it five years ago. It's impossible to work up forecasts for any area or community without having to assume a steadily growing percentage of government workers among the population. The office organization of the EC is gradually taking over all activities on the planet, just as it wound up taking over all controls, even down on the civic level, some twelve years ago. My calculations show that within as little as another thirty years all possible decision-making apparatus will be in the hands of the EC organization, down through its local offices. From then on, we'll be frozen into a pattern with some fourteen percent of the total population as an effective aristocracy and the rest as —nothing."

"Nothing?" said Carwell. "What do you mean by nothing? People with no rights at all? Slaves?"

"Not even that," said Maea. "The other eighty-six percent will simply be an unnecessary excess, requiring feeding and care but having no purpose for existing at all. Slaves aren't necessary nowadays; machinery is much more efficient and reliable."

"And what will happen to this excess, according to your calculations?" Rico asked.

"I can't calculate beyond that point," Maea said. "I can only guess."

"Let me guess for you," said Rico. "The excess eighty-six percent of population will be an encumbrance. Some means—undoubtedly some humane means—will be found to allow it to disappear."

Carwell's face sagged.

"No," he said, shaking his head. "No, no. I can't believe that."

"The idea upsets you, Morgan?" said Rico. "That's because your ethics are at work again. From where I sit, an end result like that isn't only logical, it's inevitable. I don't find it particularly upsetting, but then I'm not a Man of Good Will."

Carwell did not respond, and a small silence took over the group.

"Well," said Et, breaking it. "How about it? Do all of you want to have a hand at trying to change that future?"

Carwell, breathing raggedly, turned to confront Et.

"What does this have to do with you and us, then?" he demanded. "Why get us together to tell us these things?"

"Because I can use you," Et said. "I told you what I want, security and safety for Wally and myself. I can only be sure of that if I have something to hold over the head of the bureaucracy. As a system it's got one Achilles' heel— its aim is stasis, the maintenance of the status quo. That means its members keep their position in its hierarchy by playing by the rules. Only they can't always have played by the rules, or they'd be idealists and angels themselves. Somewhere there's information I can hold over their heads, in case they ever attempt to move against Wally and me. Help me get it, and any fallout—any information we find

that I don't need—you can have to put to your own use or
Mogow use or whatever, and good luck to you."

"Why should we help you?" Maea said levelly. "Why
not help ourselves to any information that's available?"

"Because it won't be available to you without me," said
Et. "I'm the R-Master, remember? I've already got an idea
of what I'm after—and I'll be keeping that idea to myself
unless you work with me. How about it?"

"I'm with you, of course," said Rico.

Al did not say anything. But then he did not need to say
anything. He just matched glances with Et for a second.

"Yes," said Maea, after a fraction of a moment. "Of
course I'll help."

"My God, yes," said Carwell.

"All right," said Et. "You realize it means that you
follow my lead, not that of your local chapter of the
Mogows?"

Maea and Carwell nodded.

"Fine," said Et. He turned to the secretary. "Rico, will
you get in touch with Lee Malone again? Tell him I'd like
to bring some friends to see him tonight."

Rico stood up. In the process of standing, he lost the air
of authority that had enfolded him while he sat and appeared merely the obliging secretary once more.

"Yes, Mr. Ho," he said.

He went inside the building. In a few moments he was
back. "I'm sorry, Mr. Ho," he said. "Master Malone says to
remind you you were told when you could see him next."

"Call him back," said Et. "Tell him I already know
everything he can tell me, and I've got a few things he
doesn't know to tell *him*."

Rico went back inside. This time, he did not come out
again. But after perhaps three minutes, the phone built into

the table beside Et chimed and spoke in the secretary's voice. "Mr. Ho," it said, "Master Malone says he'll expect you and your friends at seven P.M., San Diego time."

This time, the Southern California evening was milder; the last flush of sunset was still alive in the western sky, if barely so, as the five of them walked up the driveway toward Malone's front door.

"I want us to talk to him alone," Et said to Rico. "Can you keep his secretary occupied, or get him out of the way, so we can be sure he's not listening in?"

"Master Malone has no secretary," said Rico. "There's a maintenance team which comes in during the day, but it leaves before five P.M. The whole house is automated, and unless he has house guests Lee Malone is alone evenings."

"He's a real hermit," said Et.

"No, Mr. Ho. He often has house guests, and he always goes to places where they know him and where EC security has been provided."

A sudden shiver passed through Et. Borne up on the excitement of the last few days, he had been able to shove his bodily ill feeling into the background. But now a small night breeze out of the warm evening made him shake, and all at once the new discomforts and weaknesses that were always with him made themselves noticed. Suddenly, he was keenly conscious of his own mortality.

"That's right, you said something about there always being the one crazy individual, the psychotic assassin, to worry about."

"Yes," said Rico. "Any R-Master can be the peg on which to hang an irrational hatred or an irrational need for vengeance."

Et's own secret feelings toward Maea came uncomfortably back into his mind. These, like his physical troubles, had been pushed out of the forefront of his thoughts the last few days. Now they were back.

They were all at the front door now. It opened before they could knock, and Malone looked out at them from the opening, whiskers bristling.

"Brought a whole crowd, did you?" he said. "All right, all right, bring them in!"

They passed into the interior of the structure, and Malone led them to the room with the fireplace where he had talked to Et before.

"All right," he said, when they had all been introduced to him and were seated in a rough circle before the now-cold fireplace. "What's this all about, Etter?"

"To begin with," said Et, "can you tell me how long you were out, after you had your R-47?"

"Oh, ho!" crowed Malone. "No, you don't! You got in here to see me by promising to tell me things, not ask me questions."

"Well, then, I'll answer that question myself," Et said. "The answer is, you don't know. But it was a long time— a matter of days and perhaps weeks."

Malone glared at him.

"What makes you think so?"

"The same thing that makes me think you're a lousy biochemist."

Malone continued to glare, but this time he said nothing. Et turned to Carwell.

"Morgan," he said, "R-47 has been under research, constantly, since it was first discovered, hasn't it?"

"Yes, of course," said Carwell. "What I laid out for you to read from the library machine wasn't a fraction of the work that's been done on it."

"Still, even with that, the work of one man with R-47 isn't to be found in the library machines at all."

Carwell blinked.

"I don't understand," he said.

"Master Malone, here," said Et, turning back to Malone, "has been studying R-47, mainly at night, for nearly forty years. Somewhere in or under this house there's a laboratory that would make your eyes bug out—aren't I right, Malone? The only problem has been that, as I say, he's a lousy biochemist."

"Etter Ho," said Malone grimly, "you've got the kind of tongue that cuts the throat below it."

"I'm not worried," Et said. "If there's one thing you'll have made sure of, it's that this place of yours is completely bug-proof as far as the EC's concerned. The only way what I say could get carried beyond these walls is if you or any of these others with me were to repeat it, and they won't. I'm sure of that."

"I'm not," said Malone.

"No. And that's why you've made the mistake of keeping your secret all these years." Et turned to the others. "Let me tell you a story. There was a time when the research being done on R-47 was serious investigation."

"*Was* a time?" said Maea.

"That's right. But for nearly forty years," Et went on, "the reams of reports turned out by the researchers on R-47 have been mainly a reworking of old efforts, old efforts that were already known to lead nowhere. What wasn't a reworking of lost causes was nothing-work, simply a going through the motions of research to justify grants, salaries, and appointments."

"I can't believe that!" exclaimed Carwell. "Are you sure? Have you read all the work that's been done on R-47 in the last forty years? And if so, when did you get the time to do it during the last week?"

"No," said Et, "I haven't read it all. I've read enough to see the pattern. Let me remind you again that we're dealing with a human tyranny and down-to-earth causes and effects. It's not hard to point research into a blind alley and keep it there, if you have authority and control of the funds. For forty years the EC has simply subsidized the incompetent and venal among R-47 researchers. Anyone with ability found himself or herself crowded out."

"Why?" It was Maea demanding "What makes you think so?"

"I'll tell you why I think they've done it—and the fact they've done it is a matter of record, if you look at the record closely—they had to do it because something about that particular R-47 discovery scared the bureaucracy. It must have turned up something they thought was a threat to their system. And so effective research was stopped, even though the appearance of research was allowed to continue."

"You realize," said Maea crisply, "that you're talking about the sort of conspiracy that would be too large to keep under wraps."

"Not necessarily," broke in Rico. "Bureaucrats in a working system don't need to conspire. They're like spiders sitting at points on a community web. If one of them starts doing something for the good of the web, the vibrations ravel along the strands and the rest of them, following their spider nature, start helping—all without any direct spider-to-spider communication whatsoever."

Malone jerked his head about to look at Rico.

"Who're you?" the older man demanded. "I thought he said you were his secretary, his EC-assigned secretary."

"That too," said Rico. "But at the moment the post is only a cover for the more important business at hand."

"The point is," said Et, looking at Malone, "you were out of action for several weeks; but when you came completely to yourself, you were different from other R-Masters up until that time; you didn't have any of the uncomfortableness all the others complained about. You got curious about that later on and found out you'd been kept under longer than any other R-Master then alive. Then you began to find out that R-Masters after you were acting just like the earlier ones had. And they weren't being kept under for days following their injection. So you guessed that something new had been tried out on you, and it had worked."

He paused. Malone said nothing.

"That was a good guess. But then," said Et, "you tried to find out on your own what had been done to you—and that was a bad decision."

"Why?" said Maea.

"Because R-47 doesn't change anyone, as far as his basic character goes," Et said. He was still holding his gaze steady on Malone. "That's why we haven't had any great creative geniuses among the R-Masters. Whatever R-47 does to a human, it can't make bricks without straw. None of the people who've become R-Masters so far were creative geniuses to begin with, so they haven't become such as Masters either. Malone never had any flair for biochemical research. He was a hard-engineering-type tinkerer. But he tried to duplicate a breakthrough in R-47 biochemistry all by himself. It's in that sense I say he's a lousy biochemist. It's no wonder he's gotten nowhere in forty years."

"Do you think one other—even *one* other person—

could be involved in something like that," demanded Malone, "and the EC wouldn't find out?"

"Certainly," said Et. He waved his hand at the others he had brought with him. "That's why I put this team together. Of course, you've got to move fast, if a team is involved. The trick is not to duplicate research but to find out where the results of the original research went and get hold of it."

"But what good will that do anyone?" Carwell asked.

"The EC buried that knowledge," Et said. "It had to be highly dangerous to them for some reason, and if we find the knowledge we can find the reason. The one thing that's certain about R-Masters is that we're good problem solvers, and we've got two R-Masters here."

"EC has sixty more," gibed Malone.

"Doped to the eyes or harnessed to other problems," said Et. "Besides, can you see EC trusting any of the other Masters with the same knowledge we've got? For some reason they're scared stiff of R-47 graduates like you and me having a clear mind in a comfortable body."

He paused, as if waiting, but Malone sat silent.

"Come on," said Et. "You've tried it forty years your way. What have you got to lose? Try it my way for forty days."

"Or otherwise you'll let them know about my lab? Is that it? Oh, well," snarled Malone, "why not? Might as well be hung for a sheep as a lamb. But what do you need me for?"

"I think you know more about the Men of Good Will than anyone else on the planet," said Et. "I think you flaunted the fact that you approved of them as part of your pretended eccentricity—to cover you in your real contacts with them. You planned to use them if you found what you were looking for in the R-47, to use them as troops to get whatever you found to the other R-Masters. All right, I need troops now—to get at the place where the results of the further R-47 research has been stored. Because it'll be the same place that holds a lot of information I want."

"What for?" demanded Malone.

"To hold as a club over the EC and force them to leave me alone, and my brother as well—once he's revivified. Outside of that, I've got no interest in what's hidden by the EC. You can use the research information to help other R-Masters, or the Mogows, or anything else you want; that's up to you. We'll just be working together for separate but mutual benefits."

"Well, why didn't you say so to begin with?"

"Malone," said Et wearily, "will you stop playing word games? I don't have that much physical strength and patience left over, these days."

9

The director of the home in which Wallace Gunther Ho had spent his last days led Et, with Rico and Morgan Carwell, down to a shiny subcellar in which were what looked like eight metal tanks about a meter and a half thick and two and a half meters in length.

"This is essentially a temporary holding room for cryogenic patients," said the director. He was a slim, quick-moving man in his mid-fifties with sparse, straight gray hair. "Anyone who reaches a terminal point in our institution is kept encapsuled in his room until he or she can be moved to more permanent storage quarters or otherwise taken care of. In the case of Wallace, we've delayed beyond the usual time because of Master Ho's new situation and the fact that he might have special directions for us."

"Glad you did," said Et. Irrationally, he was relieved

that the metal enclosure had no window, so that he did not have to look at Wally's face Even though Wally was dead, Et felt the cold finger of guilt under his breastbone at the thought of what he intended

"Mr. Ho," said Rico, "feels that his brother would approve the use of his brother's body in a medical experiment which may be of benefit to all the race."

"I'm sure," said the director. "That is, when Wallace was here, he wasn't in condition to discuss such matters with me, but I'm sure Master Ho, knowing his brother, would know what Wallace would want."

He turned to Carwell.

"Doctor?" he said. "I suppose you'd like to check over the unit and the terminal patient?"

"Yes, I'd better," said Carwell.

The director reached for a door which opened in the side of the metal capsule by which they were all standing. Et turned away, pretending to examine the room at large and the other capsules, as Carwell, with the director, put their heads together over the opening.

Rico followed at Et's elbow.

"Trouble," he murmured beside Et's right ear.

"Trouble?" muttered Et, without turning his head. "What trouble?"

"I don't know any details yet," Rico said. "But I have a few illegal and privately built warning systems of my own. One just went off, the one that's concerned with EC authority."

"Wilson maybe?" said Et.

"No," answered Rico. "Or rather, not necessarily. Wilson is only one man. The warning I get comes whenever there is some EC central computer action concerning either yourself or myself. Somewhere in the bureaucracy someone has filed a report or asked a permission concerning one or both of us—a report or permission labeled Classified, Secret, or above."

"What's above Secret?"

"That," said Rico, "I've never been able to learn. But there's at least one higher classification. I myself have gained access to all Classified and Secret data; but I found evidence in the central computer of other data I could not tap. Probably the information we're after about R-47 would be among that other data."

"Master Ho!"

It was the director, in the far part of the room. Et turned and saw that Wally's capsule was now on an energized grav table and floating free.

"I'm sorry, Master Ho," called the director, "but you'll have to leave before us. I'm required to be the last one out of this room at all times. Regulations, you know."

"All right," said Et.

Followed by Rico, he joined Carwell, who was steering the grav table with Wally's capsule. They went out the door together and up the slideway beyond. Behind them, Et heard the heavy metal door of the cryogenic room boom shut, and a few seconds later the director caught up with them, to ride along the slideway on the opposite side of the capsule from Et.

"Did you ever stop to think," Et said to him, "what it would be like if we cut down on the number of regulations? Not did away with them entirely, you understand, just cut down on them."

The director laughed.

"Only criminals break regulations," he said, "so I assume no one but criminals would want there to be less regulations than there are. After all, what else holds civilization together?"

"But what if we did cut down?" Et asked.

The director stared at him across the coffin for a moment and then laughed again.

"You have to be joking, Master Ho," he said.

"Oh, yes," said Et. "I'm joking."

They went on up to the director's office, where there were forms to be thumbprinted and signed by which Wally's frozen entity was formally released to Et. Then they floated the capsule out of the institution and down to the dock at the foot of the grounds. Et had planned to use the same trip to Hawaii to arrange intercontinental shipment for the *Sarah* to his island, and a whim had led him to sail the *Sarah* to the institution to pick up what was left of Wally.

"You shouldn't take regulations too lightly, Mr. Ho," said Rico quietly, as they left the building behind them. "Among other things, they keep you alive."

"I could feed myself if I had to," said Et.

"I'm not talking about your perquisites as an R-Master," said Rico. "Or even about the Citizen's Basic Allowance you got before you took the R-47. The world under the Earth Council is like one big piece of working machinery, and regulations are the parts of that machine. The EC won't break regulations because they don't want anyone to tamper with the machinery, even themselves. As long as you don't tamper either, they'll put up with you in the hope you'll eventually slip and get crushed in the gears on your own. It would be easy enough for the bureaucracy to quietly kill off all the Masters and end R-47 if they were willing to break regulations themselves. But they won't, except as a last resort; the machinery justifies their own existence. It's their god, and its parts are holy."

"Hmm," said Et. Rico's words seemed to ring and reecho in his mind with an importance he could not at first pin down; then it came to him. What the smaller man was telling him was a typical example of the fact that intelligence—call it intellectual capacity—alone could be helpless in a situation where knowledge or experience was required. Rico knew the EC and the bureaucracy with a knowledge Et would be hard put to duplicate. For the first time, Et considered the unusual value of the other man to his plans and thought about what it would be like if he had to do without Rico—either immediately or later on.

It would not be good if too much depended on any one person except Et himself. In this world of regulations, complications, and hidden values, what if Rico was not the ally he seemed? What if the secretary was actually an agent put among them by the very bureaucracy they had come to oppose? Et was deep in thought by the time they reached the docks, so deep he did not at first notice the men in the white jackets with the white, pencil-barreled, laser pistols clipped to their waists who came forward to meet them as they approached the *Sarah*.

"Master Ho?" said the one on the right. Et stopped and found himself looking down at a card case the armed man held open before him, an identification plaque within. "We're Field Examiners of the Auditor Corps of the EC. Mr. St. Onge, one of the full auditors of that department, would appreciate it if you could come along with us now for a few words with him."

"Why?" demanded Et.

"I'm afraid I don't know, sir," said the Field Examiner, putting his identity plaque away in a pocket. "But I assume it's important."

"I can't come right now," Et said. "I have to take my brother in his cryogenic capsule to safe quarters on my island—"

Rico drew in his breath between his teeth in something like a faint warning hiss.

"I'm sure," said the Field Examiner, "we can ensure the well-keeping of your brother in his capsule while you visit the auditor. We really must insist you come with us now, Master Ho. We have an atmosphere ship waiting. Auditor St. Onge is in Mexico City."

He turned and pointed to an amphibious atmosphere ship rocking on the waves at the end of the dock.

"What do you mean, you must insist?" said Et. "I've got normal freedom of movement, I suppose? I'm not under arrest—or am I? If so, let's see your warrant."

"I don't know of any warrant for you at the moment, Master Ho," said the Field Examiner, in the same unvaryingly polite tones. "But I believe that if it should be necessary we might find when we arrived at the auditor's offices that a warrant had, indeed, been issued."

"Some time since, I suppose?"

"Yes indeed, sir. Some time since."

Et looked around.

"My brother in his capsule, Mr. Rico Erm, and Dr. Carwell, here, all are going to have to come with me."

"I'm sure," said the Field Examiner, "that Auditor St. Onge would be the first to insist that you have anyone you wanted with you."

"All right " said Et.

They went out and boarded the atmosphere ship. There was a small but adequate lounge inside, and the trip to Mexico City took less than an hour. It had been morning when they left the dock. It was just past 1 P.M. when they dropped down into the courtyard landing pad of the EC Western Hemisphere Center, which these days occupied most of the suburb of Gustavo A. Madero.

Here, however, Et was separated from Rico, Carwell, and the capsule containing Wally. Politely but inexorably, the Field Examiners explained that the others must wait aboard the atmosphere ship. Et was conducted alone into the surrounding buildings.

Patrick St. Onge met Et in the lounge room of an office suite that looked outward on a very large swimming pool in which some sort of water relay race was being held. Et found him standing behind the weather shield of air flowing upward across a wide window opening and gazing down at the swimmers fifteen meters below.

"Well, Et!" said St. Onge, turning to face him as Et came up flanked by the Field Examiners. "Good of you to come. I've been looking forward to seeing you again!"

"I got the impression from these two," said Et, "that there'd be a warrant found existing for my arrest if I didn't."

"You what?" St. Onge turned upon the two field men. "What regulation gave you the authority to hint at anything like that? How the hell dare you approach a Master that way?"

"Sir," began the one who had spoken to Et on the dock. "Procedures—"

"God damn your procedures," snapped St. Onge. "Did you or did you not know Mr. Ho was an R-Master?"

"Yes, sir, we knew."

"Then there's no excuse. Get out of here."

They left. The whole interchange of words had rung falsely on Et's ear, like dialogue in a badly acted play.

St. Onge turned back to Et. "I don't know what good an apology will do," he said. "But please forgive me. These idiots they're training for field work—give them a plaque and a handgun and they think they've got all the authority of the Council itself. When I was in the field, we used our heads."

"And only threatened to arrest people who weren't R-Masters?" said Et.

St. Onge burst out laughing.

"Well," he said, "at least you can joke about it. But really, I am sorry something like this had to happen. I did need to talk to you; regulations require it. But there wasn't any need to march you here under guard."

"It's actually business, then, not social—your wanting to see me?"

"I'm afraid so. After we met at the Milan Tower, I asked if I couldn't be assigned to your file. We all have to carry a certain number of files, spread out among various categories of citizens, and it's much easier to keep audit on someone you like. Much easier when something comes up and you have to talk to him."

"Do you talk to most of the citizens whose files you handle?" Et asked.

"Lord, no," said St. Onge. "Where would I find the time? No, for most citizens, even a full audit is a once-in-a-lifetime thing. But as a citizen's expenditures go up, as his share of the GWP becomes larger, more and more attention has to be paid to the file—by regulations. For perhaps half a million people in the world, a yearly full audit is automatic. And for perhaps five hundred or so, there's a running audit being processed in the central computer at all times. We call it a 'keeping' audit. You're in that category, Et, and what it means is that I get a daily report on any expenditures of yours that exceed the estimates forecast according to your spending profile."

"I see," said Et. "What have I done now? Or are you thinking about the GWP units I gambled away in Hong Kong?"

"No, no, of course not," said St. Onge, "We expect the new R-Masters to get a bit extravagant as they feel their way into their new life. But—sit down, why don't we?"

They seated themselves opposite each other.

"That's better," said St. Onge. "No, the little problem that's come up now doesn't actually deal with any current expenses of yours. We'll be wanting to run a special forecast of expenses, if this attempt of yours to revive your brother extends into more extensive work and research than is covered by the compassionate funds—"

"Who told you about that?" demanded Et. "I only signed the waiver of responsibility a little over a week ago."

"But it had to be filed—the waiver form," said St. Onge, with an odd, sudden, flashing smile that was like the heatless flicker of lightning. "Any time you deal with forms, the information goes to the central computer, and from the central computer to your file in my office, of course."

"Of course," said Et. "You'll have to excuse me. I've been used to living without everything I did being recorded and annotated."

"You mean before you became an R-Master?" said St. Onge. "Sorry to disillusion you, but even then you had papers to fill out every time your ship entered or cleared a harbor or you drew your allowance or purchased something. Also, the citizens who had to do with you had their own forms and records to make. I've no doubt the central computer could give us a day-to-day diary of your actions since you were school age. Would you like me to ask for a printout on that sometime?"

"No, thanks," said Et. He loosened the neck of his jacket. The room was warmer than he had noticed it being on his arrival.

"Be glad to. No trouble at all; you might find it amusing."

"No," said Et. "You were going to tell me why you wanted to talk to me."

"Oh, that. Yes," said St. Onge. "As you know, R-Masters can have pretty much anything they want. But we have a responsibility not to waste funds beyond the Master's own needs and desires. Now, you've happened to make some rather peculiar acquaintances since you had the R-47 reaction. I don't know if you're aware of it, but the man you chose as a personal physician over Dr. Hoskides, Morgan Carwell, belongs to an organization called the Men of Good Will. So does Maea Tornoy, whom you asked for. And of course Master Lee Malone has shown a long-time interest in that organization, among his other interests."

"Am I supposed to have fallen among dangerous companions?" Et asked. "Is that it?"

"Dangerous?" St. Onge laughed. "Good God, no! Organizations capable of actual subversion against the EC are a practical impossibility nowadays. Not only does the EC know immediately if anyone becomes a member of any group or organization at all, but of course it controls that individual's wages or allowance and through ordinary day-to-day records can tell exactly what he's doing and pick him up the moment he attempts to infringe regulations."

"He'd be smart not to infringe regulations, then," said Et.

"Of course. And that's why almost none of these odd-group members do," said St. Onge. "Of course, if they don't infringe regulations, they don't do any harm and we don't need to worry about them. So as a matter of fact we don't have to worry—about anyone but the actual criminal regulation-breaker. But even people like that are no real problem. They may get away with breaking regulations for a little while, but eventually we catch up with them too."

"In the Sunset Hut at Hong Kong," said Et, "I saw people betting on a fencing match. But the fencers were using sharpened weapons, and one man was killed. I saw him killed."

"Oh, you've seen the matches?" said St. Onge. "Actually, something like that lies in a sort of gray area as far as the regulations go, though of course we keep a quiet but steady eye on it. The duelists are all volunteers, of course. The gambling managements like to foster the rumor that people are kidnapped or drugged and forced to duel. But drugging, of course, we'd crack down on right away; and, in fact, who could be forced? It's impossible to lose more credit gambling than you have, these days, with instantaneous record-keeping. So there couldn't be any such thing as paying off losses to the casino by risking your life the way legend has it that some duelists are doing."

"But who'd volunteer for something like that?" Et asked.

"Why, people bent on suicide, for example," said St.

Onge. "As long as they register the intent to do away with themselves, it's all perfectly according to regulations. Or—more common—someone who considers himself a very good fencer and wants to risk an encounter with real weapons to test his skill. Again, if he's registered his intent, that makes the duel simply a dangerous sport. Someone like that, matched with another such sportsman who's equally skilled, or a would-be suicide, untrained, matched with another like himself, breaks no regulations."

St. Onge gave another of his heatless smiles.

"In fact," he said, "I might tell you that I've tried the sport once or twice myself. I'm really rather good as a fencer. Do you fence?"

"No," said Et.

"Ah," said St. Onge.

"All right then," said Et. "Since the Men of Good Will are harmless, why bring me here to talk to me about them?"

"Oh, just a word of caution," St. Onge said. "As I say, we want the R-Master to have all the funds he wants. On the other hand—and I'm afraid my department has had to crack down on Master Malone in this respect—we can't have him becoming a funnel by which funds reach other citizens, or citizen groups, that aren't really entitled to them. You understand, I'm sure. . . . Is something the matter? Are you all right?"

"Warm in here, isn't it?" said Et.

The room about him, it seemed to Et, had become steadily warmer since his arrival. He had become accustomed, in the week since he had first woken from the R-47 reaction, to ignoring the minor discomforts to which the drug had rendered him liable. But this present oppressive heat was raising his feelings of illness above their normal level. He felt feverish and weak. His customary small headache was a pounding sledgehammer just behind his temples, and the air he drew into his lungs felt thick and unnatural.

"Is it?" said St. Onge, jumping to his feet. "I hadn't noticed. Let me open the window."

He stepped to the window and punched at the control button in the center of its sill. The curtain of upflowing air died, and a cool breeze from the outside atmosphere swept into the room. At first its chill touch was a relief to Et, but in seconds all heat fled from him and he began to shiver uncontrollably.

"Good Lord, you *are* having trouble," said St. Onge, watching him. "You should remember how frail you are nowadays. Maybe we'd better get you back to your island as soon as possible."

"Don't you," said Et, between teeth he barely kept from chattering, "don't you feel that the air from outside is cold?"

"No." St. Onge shook his head. He stepped across, touched the window control, and immediately the room started to heat up for Et again. "To tell you the truth, no. Not really. I'm afraid it's that R-47 reaction making you vulnerable to little changes in temperature like this. Damned shame, but you'll just have to get used to keeping yourself carefully protected at all times from now on. That's a good reason by itself for your staying clear of political and other matters. You really should start letting Dr. Hoskides take care of you with the proper medicines. A lot of this sort of thing can be shunted off with the correct drugs, they tell me. You'd be much more comfortable under Hoskides' care."

"No, thanks," said Et, getting unsurely to his feet.

"Here, let me help you to the door. . . . Oh, Cele!"

Cele Partner had just appeared in the room.

"Et! What's the matter?" she cried, running to him. She put her arms around him. "Here, let me help. What's wrong?"

"The room got a little warm and then a bit too chilly for him," said St. Onge, on the other side of Et. "You're a godsend, Cele. Could you see he gets back to his ship all right? I can't leave the office. Got an appointment in a few minutes I can't break."

"Of course I'll take care of him," said Cele. "Come on, Et. Let me get you into one of the inside rooms where there's complete climate control. Then you can lie down while I arrange a way to move you without letting you have any more reactions like this."

She helped Et out of the office, a short way down the corridor, and into a small room where the temperature seemed to be within comfortable limits and there were no drafts. He was left lying on a couch, alternately shivering and sweating, until she came back with two of the armed Field Examiners—a different two from those who had brought Et here—and a floating grav surface with what looked like a transparent hood over its full length.

"I'm not going to travel in that thing!" said Et. "I can walk."

But with Cele's perfume in his nostrils, he allowed himself to be helped in under the hood. He rode back down to the atmosphere ship and, with Carwell and Rico beside him, made the trip back to the island.

He did not, however, improve as he went along. After a

while he stopped shivering and simply ran a fever that, by the time they arrived, had made him light-headed, almost drunk. He vaguely remembered being carried to a room on the same hooded grav surface that had brought him out of the EC Western Hemisphere Center.

Later yet, he was vaguely aware of being prodded and examined. But that, too, ended, and he sank into the oblivion and anesthesia of a sleep for which he was as grateful as a starving man might be for a full meal.

10

He dreamed of Cele. In the beginning, in the Milan Tower, he had been both attracted and challenged by her, but not really anything beyond that. There was something about her that seemed hidden and out of reach, so that he did not have the feeling for her he had had for other women he had known and wanted. In a way he had liked all of them; in that same way a liking for Cele was lacking in him. But this second meeting had increased the attraction and challenge she had for him. She was something like the fever that had burned him up on the way back to the island, unnatural but momentarily intoxicating.

His dreams of her after he got back to the island were confused dreams. He could not remember after he woke just what they had been. But Cele had run through them all like a darkly glittering thread leading him on beyond rational thought. Then, at last, he woke and found his dream concern for her vanished with the fever. All at once he remembered his many other concerns.

He lay on a grav bed in the room he had slept in during his first nights on the island. He felt weak but clean. Rolling on his side with an effort, he reached out to the bedside table and punched the "on" stud of the phone.

"Anyone there?" he called.

"Yes, Mr. Ho," said Rico's voice. A moment later, the secretary came in with Carwell.

"How are you feeling?" Carwell asked.

"Limp as an oyster," said Et. "Otherwise not bad. In fact, better than I've been feeling ever since I first woke up from the R-47. What happened to me?"

"It seems," said Carwell, "you caught a cold."

Et stared at him unbelievingly.

"A cold?"

"I'm afraid that's all it was," Carwell said. "Evidently because of the R-47 you react a lot more violently to small infections than I'd thought. In fact, I had to have Dr. Hoskides examine you."

"That—" Et started to sit up in bed. Carwell gently held him down.

"Don't worry. All he did was examine. You've got my word he didn't give you any medicines."

Et relaxed.

"I can't believe it," he said. "Only a cold? I felt as if I was in the last stages of . . . I don't know what."

"Dr. Hoskides said that to you, of course, the sensation of sickness would seem more pronounced. Just as, he said, you thought the room was a good deal hotter than that auditor—St. Onge, is it?—was actually keeping it; and the breeze you felt seemed a lot colder than it actually was."

"I don't believe that," said Et flatly. "I've been getting used to the way I react since I had the R-47. What I ran into in Patrick's office was a lot worse than anything I've felt so far. It was hotter and colder than normal. Either Patrick was pretending not to feel as much as I did, or else he's got a pretty powerful lack of sensitivity himself."

Carwell shook his head. He was feeling Et's forehead and checking his pulse.

"Yes," Carwell said, "you're a good bit improved. But you'd better plan on resting for a day or two."

"Oh, no." Et tried once more to force himself up into a sitting position on the side of the bed and made it this time, in spite of Carwell's pushing him back down. "We've got to move. I've got to move. There are things to do, with Wally and with the business of finding that R-47 information we want."

He checked himself suddenly, looking around at the walls.

"That reminds me," he said to Rico. "Eavesdropping of any kind is against regulations, even for the EC itself— or so I was taught. And I know you said our particular opponents like to play by the regulations. But maybe we'd better check these premises."

"For bugs?" Rico asked. "I already did, the first day I was here and every day since. None."

"All right then," said Et. He stood up and was happy to find out he was stronger than he had thought, now that he was fully awake. "I'll get dressed."

The capsule holding Wally had been moved to one wing of the buildings on the island, a wing which was now being expanded and remodeled into completely independent quarters, consisting of a revival theater, living section, and

training area for Wally, when and if he should be successfully brought back from the arrested death in which he
now lay.

"But you mustn't expect too much," Carwell said to Et,
as they moved among the workmen making the alterations. "The odds are against any revival to a reasonable
state at all—I mean, any revival above the basic immediate
level of coma. And if something better is achieved, the
most we can hope for is that he'll regain a state something
below the level of the moderate-to-severe mental deficiency he was showing at the time of his death. It's true
the act of his suicide was somewhat beyond what we
would have expected from someone with that limited
an intellectual capability—"

"I'm not hoping for any miracle," said Et harshly. "Just
reasonable results!"

He heard his own voice in his ears like the voice of
a stranger. There was something in it he had never heard
from himself before, something animal-angry.

He was out of words. They continued to walk on together over the neatly cropped lawn of the island grounds,
sloping down to the soft blue Caribbean waves. Carwell
watched him but said nothing, and after a while they came
to the docks where an atmosphere ship belonging to Et
himself rocked on the waves beside the *Sarah*, waiting. Rico
and Maea were on the docks beside it.

"What is it?" asked Et, as they came up to the other
two.

"I've found someone who knows where the secret EC
files are hidden," said Rico. "I've set up an appointment.
But the man I've found doesn't want to talk to any more
people than he has to. That means you and me, only."

"All right," said Et. He turned to Maea and Carwell.

"We'll see you as soon as we get back."

Maea put a hand on his arm.

"How are you feeling?" she asked.

"How am I? Fine," said Et. He moved away from her and the touch of her hand. The sight of Wally's capsule had reawakened his original feelings against her. "Let's go, Rico."

He led the way into the atmosphere ship, and they took off westward.

Their destination was one of those underwater sealed-dome communities in the shallow waters just off the coast of Mexico, in the Gulf of Mexico. It had begun as a retirement community, had been taken over by a new generation of young families that could not afford the units to buy private homes ashore, and had ended up as a sort of third-rate undersea resort area, which catered to people from shore with enough spare credit to buy saltwater fishing licenses.

Among other attractions grown up with the resort character of the community was a sort of amusement park on a high piece of bottom less than thirty meters from the surface. The amusement park offered underwater mazes, tank fishing, and various other entertainments, some of them in their way as seamy as the dueling gym Et had stumbled into in the Sunset Hut near Hong Kong.

"Don't look in the tank," said the young woman who was guiding them to the man with whom Rico had made the appointment.

She was a local housewife who refused to give her name, but who had been the one to meet them when they had gone to a certain restaurant according to the directions of their contract. She obviously wanted or needed the monetary units she could earn by acting as their guide, although it was clear that she despised not only what she was doing but the person to whom she was conducting them. But for some unknown reason she had apparently taken a liking to Et at first sight.

"Why not?" asked Et. They were traveling through a tube passageway, surrounded completely by the water of the thirty-meter depth in which the amusement park was located.

Before he could get an answer from her, they reached the pressure door at the end of the tube. It unsealed with a sucking sound to let them through to an area containing what looked like a swimming pool, enclosed by a high wire fence at its very edge and surrounded by bleacher seats. The seats were nearly all filled, mostly by people whose heavily suntanned skins showed them to be land dwellers and probable tourists here in the undersea community. The woman led them to the end of the first row of bleacher seats on the near side of the pool, up to a fat man of unguessable age.

The reason his age defied estimate was that he had no teeth in his mouth. Normally, people kept their adult teeth all their lives; even if his lack of them was the result of a birth defect the man could have been fitted with dentures. It therefore had to be assumed that he preferred to go around toothless. He grinned at Et and Rico with thick, pink lips between a nose and chin that almost touched.

"Which one of you's Erm?" he asked in a high-pitched voice.

"I am," said Rico.

"And your friend here, who wants to be nameless, who's he, I wonder?" The man laughed; then he sobered abruptly and jerked his head at the woman who had brought them. She turned and left.

"Have you got some place where we can talk privately?" Rico asked.

"Sure," lisped the man, "but what's your hurry? The feeding frenzy's due in a second. That's when we lift the barrier. Have a seat and watch, as my guests. I'm the manager here, you know. It won't cost you a thing."

"We don't have time," said Rico.

"You'd better have time," murmured the fat man softly and malevolently. "You'd better have time or I won't talk to you at all. After all, why should I? Sit down or get out!"

He moved over on the bench to give them room.

They sat. Looking down into the pool, Et saw it was divided in the middle by an opaque barrier. In the section farther from him half a dozen white sharks, all about four meters in length, were swimming about. In the right-hand section three bottle-nosed dolphins were darting back and forth underwater; on the bottom of their part of the tank, dead and belly up, were two more white sharks. Obviously the sharks had been introduced, perhaps one at a time, to the section containing the dolphins, and the dolphins had battered both selachians to death. Now however, as Et watched, a chute opened in the shark section and disgorged perhaps a couple of hundred kilos of bloody meat.

The sharks congregated upon it. At first they merely fed. Then abruptly, so abruptly Et suspected that some drug or chemical had been introduced to the water around them, the sharks went into a feeding frenzy, a mad swirl of sinuous bodies in which they bit and tore not only at the food but at each other.

And finally the barrier between the two sections split open, each half withdrawing into one of the underwater side walls of the pool.

It took a moment or two for the sharks to discover the dolphins. But by this time the original quantity of meat had already been gulped down, and shortly the frenzy became pool-wide. Swifter than the sharks, many times as intelligent, the dolphins evaded the threshing appetites for some minutes. But soon one of them was slashed, then another, and the beginning of the end began.

Looking away from the pool at the people in the bleachers around him, Et saw—or thought he saw—the same faces he had seen staring down at the gym floor where the two fencers dueled with sharpened weapons in the Sunset Hut, and a nausea twisted inside him.

He got up and walked away from the bleacher. A touch on his arm made him turn around. Rico and the fat man were right behind him.

"We can talk now," said the fat man. "Come on."

He led the way through a door at one end of the pool area, along another tube corridor through the undersea, and finally into a large room beyond.

This room also contained a pool, but at poolside was the furniture of a fairly complete office, including desk, office equipment, and grav-float seats. The pool here was partitioned into eight sections by transparent dividing walls that went down to the bottom and rose out of the water a good twenty feet—higher than a bottle-nose dolphin could jump, particularly with no more than three meters' depth of water in which to make its preliminary dive. At the far end of each section was a metal gate leading to a water lock and the open sea.

Each section of the pool held a dolphin. Several of these surfaced as the humans came in and swan. forward to push their heads onto the near edge of the pool by the desk

The twittering of their voices lifted in the air of the pool-side office.

"How do you like that?" said the fat man, waddling forward to drop onto a grav float behind the desk. "Sit down. No, I say, how do you like the way they come up to the edge for me like that? They've got a pretty good idea I'm going to end up shifting them into the other tank and that for some reason they'll never come back. But they still like to be talked to. And if I fell into one of those pool sections, do you think the one in there would hurt me? Never. Probably he'd try to hold me up instead, until I could climb out at the edge."

He broke off, fastening his eyes on Et.

"What's the matter with you?" he asked, adding, with a blubbery twist of his lips, "Mr. R-Master?"

Et said nothing.

"Didn't think I'd know, did you?" said the man. "But that's my business, knowing things. That's why you're here, because I know things. Well, let me tell you, Mr. R-Master, you don't impress me. I don't need you or your money or your special position. None of it makes any difference to me. All the same, I'm willing to do business."

"Good," said Rico, calmly and quietly. "Your name is Shu-shu, I'm told? And you're a free-lance ombudsman as well as being manager of this place?"

"You know what I am," said Shu-shu. He was still watching Et. "See that brown stud on my desktop, Mr. R-Master? One touch and the gates at the far ends of the sections'd be open, and the water lock would let them out. All these little prisoners of mine, they'd go free. Wouldn't you like to push that stud? But of course, I can't let you do that—not for any amount of credit."

Rico's voice was still as soft and polite as the voice of an answering service.

"I must ask for your attention, Mr. Shu-shu."

"Just Shu-shu. Never mind any titles." The fat man turned his attention finally to Rico.

"Shu-shu." Rico's voice went on as if he had never been interrupted. "It's unusual for a free-lance ombudsman to have another occupation, if he's any good at free-lancing."

"I'm pretty good." A little bit of spittle moistened Shu-shu's lips with the effort of pronouncing the p. "But this is my hobby, this place with its dolphin-shark fights. Anyway, if you don't want to trust what I can tell you, you can stroll on out of here."

"Of course," said Rico, "of course. But an FLO, a free-lance ombudsman, is someone who hires himself out to help other people, to stand in line for them, to pound on official desks for them. To help them. Naturally, he's paid, but you assume there must be some basic kindness in such an individual. You, on the other hand, seem to enjoy putting on your shark-dolphin fights."

"Mr. Erm," said Shu-shu, leaning far back on his float, "I think you're beginning to tire me out. I don't believe I want to tell you what you and your pet R-Master want to know, after all. The door's right behind you. Good-by."

Rico, however, made no attempt to get up. Instead he turned to Et.

"Sir," he said in the same polite voice, "this individual is obviously a sadist. I assume he keeps his vices within regulations or the EC would have picked him up long ago. But I think we can safely assume he wants to do business more badly than we do, not for the credit involved but because he receives a stimulation from the purveying of information, just as he receives stimulation from managing the slaughter of sea creatures that are all but human in their own right. On the other hand, our own schedule is rather tight and he's already wasted some minutes of our time. I suggest we do leave."

Et stood up.

"Wait," said Shu-shu, himself rising hastily behind the desk. "Wait."

"Perhaps, sir"—Rico glanced at Et—"we could give him another two minutes—no more?"

Et sat down. Shu-shu dropped back onto his own grav float, almost panting.

"All right, all right," he said. "All right. Of course, I don't break regulations. I don't have any information I shouldn't. But I don't have to. Being an ombudsman I hear things, from my clients and from others—"

Rico glanced at the chronometer on his left wrist.

"All right," said Shu-shu hastily, "here it is. It seems to me I've heard of certain construction, originally done very quietly about thirty years ago but added to at intervals since, under the Museum of Natural History buildings in Manhattan, New York City. Of course I've entirely forgotten where that information came to me, It might have been part of something I dreamed one night."

Rico and Et got to their feet.

"Now, if you'd like to retain me for possible help to you as a free-lance ombudsman, my retainer is five thousand units."

"A voucher will be sent to you. Not from one of us, of course," murmured Rico.

"Just as long as I get paid," said Shu-shu. He reached out and touched a white stud on his desk. "Now, just for the record, if I could record the purpose of this consultation—the purpose for which you needed me as ombudsman?"

"Yes," said Et. "I'd like to promote a regulation to make dolphins a protected species as far as their use in any shows are concerned."

Shu-shu laughed—and broke off laughing suddenly as Et reached over to press down the brown stud the other man had pointed out earlier. The stud went down under Et's finger. The gates at the far ends of the section flashed open.

Shu-shu reached with both hands for Et's finger.

"Don't try it," Et told him, "unless you want to get your face rebuilt."

Shu-shu sagged back. The dolphins were already flashing out of the water lock beyond the gates, to freedom in the open sea.

"Well, now," said Shu-shu, close to spitting as he spoke. "I'll just have to get more. And of course, you'll have to pay for them—and my losses meanwhile—or I'll take legal action. That was pretty much like robbery with a threat of violence, what you did just now. At the very least, I'll sue. I'll hit you with a civil suit unless I'm paid, and paid well!"

"Sue, then, and damn you!" said Et. He was shaking all over. He turned and walked out unsteadily, with Rico behind him.

11

The intercontinental fell to the pad on the island at precisely 10:13 A.M., local time, and two minutes later the lean, balding figure of Dr. Fernando James Garranto y Vega emerged, glittering in a full transparent oversuit and moving at a good eight-kilometers-an-hour walk.

"Mr. Ho?" he asked briskly as Et stepped forward to meet him. His voice echoed a little, coming through the breathing filter of the hood. "Come along, take me to the patient. We can talk as we go. I'm due back in São Paulo early tomorrow."

"I appreciate your coming," Et said.

"I'm glad you do. I say that not for myself but in the name of my other patients." They entered the new wing of the island buildings, where Wally's capsule was housed. "I can appreciate—I say, *appreciate*—the fact that you have good private reasons for asking me to come here for the revival rather than bringing your brother to me. But the time coming and going to your island is time spent at the expense of someone else who also needs my services."

"I repeat," said Et, "it had to be this way, and I thank you."

"Very well. Through here?" said Garranto, stepping into the outer antechamber to the operating room. "Good-by. I'll talk to you later."

The door closed behind the physician. Et stepped around to the window giving a review of both the antechambers and the revival arena beyond. He saw Garranto, standing in front of the microwave plate which was disintegrating the oversuit that had kept him germ free during his walk from the intercontinental to the operating areas. The suit gone, Garranto stepped quickly into the inner antechamber, where six other physicians were waiting for him.

"Gentlemen, I know you all, I think?" said Garranto, nodding at them. "Yes, Keyess, Tuumba, Martin . . . there's no one who hasn't worked with me before? Good. You all know your positions, then. Shall we begin?"

He led the way into the revival arena, and the complicated process began of thawing Wally, removing the special cryogenic solutions from his body, and reactivating the whole silenced symphony of his organic processes. Et stood by the window watching, not because he wanted to be there but because an obscure penitential feeling kept him where he was, until finally the once-more breathing and warm shape of his brother was floated out of the arena into the adjoining room where Wally would begin now to recover, in the next nine hours, as much of himself as there was to be recovered after his clinical death and his period of frozen suspension.

Et turned away from the window and almost fell. Abruptly, all the fatigue, the aches and pains that he had forgotten as he stood watching what was being done to Wally, came swooping back to possess him. He tottered like an old man and almost fell. A hand went around his waist, steadying him. He looked down, expecting to see Al, but it was Maea.

"Where'd you come from?" he asked thickly.

She looked at him strangely.

"I've been here watching, with you," she said.

She was helping him now, as he made his heavy, uncertain way back to his own room and his own bed surface. He fell on it at last and lay staring at the ceiling.

"You stood there too long," she said.

"Yes." He heard his own voice, talking from a long way off. "Too long. I'll get a little sleep now—a little sleep."

He heard her footsteps going away, the room dimmed, and there was the sound of a door closing. But he did not go immediately to sleep. Instead, he hung there, on the precipice lip of slumber, realizing finally that his determination to bring Wally back to life had been more than a desire; it had been a compulsion. If the world had been allowed to get away with killing Wally, it would have proved itself a real enemy after all, and Et would be deeply guilty of letting it conquer his brother while he stood aside. But now everything would be all right. He had paid back . . . what? His exhausted mind could not form the idea of what he had accomplished. It was something like paying an old debt. Something like that. . . .

He awoke abruptly.

For a moment he did not know where he was. Then

memory came back and it seemed to him that he had just closed his eyes a moment ago. But the room was full of morning light, and Rico was standing over him.

"What—?" Et said.

"I'm sorry to wake you," said Rico. "But Dr. Garranto is leaving, and he wants to speak to you before he goes."

"Speak to me." Et propped himself up on one elbow, running a hand over his numb and bristled face. "How long have I been sleeping?"

"Fourteen hours."

"Fourteen!" Et's mind jolted into full awareness. "Wally —how's Wally?"

A little change passed across the polite features of Rico.

"Dr. Garranto wants to give you a full report."

"Oh." Et swung his legs over the edge of the bed and sat up. "Where is he?"

"Just outside the door. If you don't mind, he'd like to come right in. He's eager to leave."

"Fine," said Et. "Let him in, then."

He rubbed the last of the sleepiness out of his eyes as Rico went to the door of the bedroom and opened it to let Garranto in and himself out. As the door closed, the narrow-bodied doctor strode briskly over to where Et waited, pulled up a chair, and sat down so that they faced each other.

"How's Wally?" asked Et.

Garranto did not answer at once. For a second he merely stared directly into Et's eyes.

"Mr. Ho," he said, "I want you to understand something. I'm a highly trained physician in a medical area where there are never enough highly trained men. I don't have enough time to handle all the patients I'd like to handle, let alone involve myself in anything outside my work with patients."

Et nodded. Garranto's formal and oblique answer to his question had started a small uneasy feeling inside him, but he repressed it.

"Fair enough," said Et. "What about Wally?"

"We had a very successful revivification in the case of your brother," said Garranto. "He responded excellently. Physically, he could hardly be in better shape. Mentally, I'm sorry to say, the case was otherwise."

The uneasy feeling blossomed inside Et.

"How bad . . ." he began, but the words stuck in his throat.

"I'm afraid"—the voice of Garranto tolled in his ears— "that mentally there was no effective recovery at all. In short, I'm sorry to tell you that your brother is in almost a state of coma, from which we can't hope to rouse him."

Darkness roared in the back of Et's mind. He felt the room tilting about him and then felt himself steadied by the strong hand of the physician.

"Hold on, there!" Garranto was saying. "Hold on. How do you feel?"

"It didn't work," muttered Et. He was conscious of himself in the room, with Garranto facing him; but with another part of his mind he was falling, endlessly falling, down into nothingness. Opening out forever before him was the eternity in which Wally would never recover; for the first time he faced the fact that he had never really accepted that possibility. From the start he had ignored all warnings; inwardly he had been sure that Wally would be brought back, not merely to warmth and life but to his old ability and powers.

"No," he said, pushing Garranto's supporting hand from him, "I'm all right. I'd been hoping—but I should have known better, of course."

"No," said Garranto strangely. "No, you shouldn't have known better."

Et stared at him.

"What do you mean?"

"I mean, damn it, that the odds were there, the odds against your brother being returned to mental normality!" snapped Garranto. "Your own physician must have warned you—Carwell—and I warned you; but in my own mind, Mr. Ho, I actually gave your brother a better than even chance, a good deal better than even chance. He was young. The death had been sudden and entirely physical in induction. He had been cryoed immediately. The odds should have been good to return him to normal activity both mental and physical."

Et laughed without humor.

"Why tell me this now?" he said.

"Because." Garranto's tone of voice put a period after the word. Reaching into the side pocket of his jacket, he came out with a small transparent bottle with a heavy stopper. Within were a few cubic centimeters of what looked like a pale amber liquid.

"I told you I was a busy man," he said. "I've got no time to answer lawyers' questions and sit in courts of justice, no matter how good the cause. When your brother failed to respond mentally to the normal procedure, I did a spinal tap and found traces of a substance which I have never encountered before in the spinal fluid of anyone following a R-47 injection—even in the case of someone who, like your brother, had had a bad reaction to the drug.

I don't know what this substance is, and I don't want to know. But it appears, among other things, to inhibit the production and liberation of acetylcholine at the postganglionic parasympathetic terminals of the nervous system.'

He got to his feet, walked across to a window, and punched the stud that set it sliding open. He opened the container and poured its contents out into the open air.

Unable to move, Et watched.

"As I said," Garranto went on, coming back across the room to stand before him, "I've got my work to do; I'll deny ever having this conversation with you, if it comes down to that. But if I was a betting man, I'd bet that your brother had something administered to him other than the normal R-47 formula, and that other, whatever it was, was responsible for his mental decay and the fact that now he'll never recover from his present state."

Garranto looked grimly at Et.

"Forgive me," he said, "but nothing I or anyone else can do can help your brother now. Good-by."

He turned and went out.

Et still sat.

There was no darkness roaring in the back of his mind now. There was only a spreading numbness of realization, behind the leaping conclusions of his own R-47–stimulated mind, flogged into extreme activity by the brutal surge of adrenalin called forth by the information that Wally had been deliberately destroyed.

Of course. His mind leaped, as in magic seven-league boots, taking great and certain strides from evidence to conclusion and on to further conclusions. Wally was known to be a Mogow. What special knowledge he might have had, or whether he had been only an experimental subject as far as the EC bureaucracy was concerned, did not matter now. What mattered was only the fact of what they had done to him—and what Et would guide him, or the shell of him, to do in return.

No longer was it a matter of setting up a situation in which he and Wally would be left alone by bureaucracy and Mogow alike. Now it was a matter of Wally's living-dead hand which would bring retribution upon the EC Council itself.

12

Three days later Rico was waiting for Et in the workroom that had been set up for the private use of Et and himself. A large architectural image was three-dimensionally depicted on the viewscreen of a tilted grav-table surface against one wall.

"Mr. Ho—" began Rico as soon as Et appeared.

"Damn it!" exploded Et. "Why can't you call me by my first name like everyone else?"

Rico stared at him for perhaps a second.

"I can, of course," he said. "But to be truthful, I feel more comfortable speaking to you formally. You'd rather I called you Et?"

"No, no," said Et wearily. "Forgive me. Call me anything you want. Is this the plan of the area under the Museum of Natural History that has the files we're after?"

"Essentially," said Rico. He picked up a long thin light-pencil and began indicating areas as he mentioned them.

"This is the elevator shaft down to it, this is the entrance, and the files are here. Actually, what you're looking at is a composite rendering, built up from a number of sources of information. To begin with, what Shu-shu told us was no more than a possibility. I've checked it, however, from a number of angles, at several removes—for example, from old records of New York subway tunnels, comparison figures over the years of the number and people going in and out of the museum each day, records of repairs within the museum itself and of the mechanical equipment involved, and so forth—all things which can be safely examined from public sources without alerting EC's central computer to the fact that anyone is interested in what's underneath the museum."

"Then this is only what you believe it looks like—if it's there?" asked Et.

"It's a little more than that," said Rico. "Enough things check so that we can be pretty sure it's there, all right. Call its existence certain. Otherwise the amount of coincidence involved in the dovetailing of information is beyond belief. It's there, and it's quite a simple layout —which helps protect it. It's simply a secret additional subfloor beneath the museum, with files of records on old-fashioned mm—multiplex microfiche. It has one drop-tube elevator with its upper entrance hidden within an electronically guarded vault entered from the office of one of the museum officials. That official is the only one on the museum staff who knows about the subfloor and the files. All requests for information go directly to him. He goes down, copies the necessary records, and brings the information up again."

"I see," said Et.

"I should add," said Rico, "that the rock around the sub-basement—and it's sunk in the rock that underlies all Manhattan—is loaded with sensors."

"All right," said Et. "How do we get to the files?"

"We were expecting the answer to that question from you, Mr. Ho."

"From me?"

"Yes, sir," said Rico. "You're the Master. You have the problem-solving ability. Frankly, I don't see any way into that sub-basement without our being identified and traced back here, eventually—even if we should manage to get away with the information we want. But if there is a way, someone like you would be the one to find it."

"I see," said Et.

"Yes, Mr. Ho. Shall I leave you to think about it?"

"All right. I can try, at least."

Rico went out. Et was left gazing at the rendering of the sub-basement. He touched the controls of the screen and brought up an image of the museum itself, above the sub-basement. To the right of that image, he punched for a display of data on the museum employee who alone had access to the file room; following this, he asked for information on the connection between this man and the EC itself and on the route by which information was channeled through the single individual both to and from the files.

The information displayed was detailed and complete. Rico had done a good job of setting it up. Et pulled up a grav-float seat and sat down, gazing at the screen and thinking.

When Rico had first left him, he had not felt confident. Wally's revival had emptied him emotionally. His optimism and enthusiasm were drained away, and he skirted the edges of a pit of depression in which the various discomforts of his body would become overpowering.

Now, however, as he read the display and studied the rendering of the sub-basement file room, interest began to kindle in him. Little by little, his depression and the small complaints of his body were pushed into the background of his consciousness. His thoughts expanded to encompass all the information available on the problem and consider it.

The process was self-feeding. As his interest rose, he found himself responding physically, as he had responded during the gambling session at the Sunset Hut. Self-adrenalized, he began to lift on as strong an emotional push upward as the downward pushes that had sickened him after seeing the fencers and the dolphins. His discomforts began to be crowded off into nonexistence; his body felt light and powerful with energy. His thoughts increased their speed, multiplied, and swelled from something like a slow trickle down a gentle slope to a cataract pouring down some steep mountainside.

He found himself up on his feet and pacing the room. His intellect burned. He rode the furious current of his thoughts as if his attention was a canoe charging among the foam and boulders of a rapids. By twos, threes, and dozens, solutions and answers to things he had wondered about all his life came pouring into him. Lost among these was the problem that had started it all, the question of how to get into the sub-basement under the museum.

He did not even wonder about that now. The problem was still there, he would get to it eventually, and when he did no serious effort would be required to solve it. More important was the sheer intoxication of cerebration. He *thought* now, with the sheer joy in pure thinking that the painter feels as color and image leap into life from his brush on the canvas or that the composer feels as notes in an order never before conceived sing back to him from the piano on which he is developing them.

In one great rush he reviewed all of Earth and its history up to the present moment. He ran his mind along the time of recorded mankind as he might have slowly stroked the sleek side of some great cat, feeling the warmth and texture of each hair as his fingers passed. He spread the present before him like a map, then added to it that third dimension built of the characters of those presently alive—the community social pressure, reaching out to create the momentum of an economic and political juggernaut that was now running wild, out of control, headed down the steepening slope of the future to inevitable destruction and ruin against the blank wall of a blind alley.

There was no way to stop that juggernaut. But it could be diverted. Just a few successive small barriers in its path, at the right points, would jolt the whole massive vehicle aside onto a different vector, one leading it down a different street, where there was no blind wall waiting—

"Et?"

He broke suddenly from the world of his thoughts to find Maea just inside the door of the room, staring at him.

"Et?" she said. "I'm sorry. I didn't mean to interrupt. But you acted as if you couldn't even see me."

"It's all right," he said automatically.

The torrent of his thoughts had not yet been checked. They were with him still, but they were being diverted around this interruption like the water of the rapids around a boulder in the riverbed.

"What do you want?" he asked her.

"I wanted to tell you about Wally," she answered. "The sensors they've got on him right now show signs he's returning to some sort of consciousness. But Et, he can't come back, can he?"

"No," Et said. "They're right. He can't possibly recover." He looked at her now with different eyes. She too had once loved Wally, he remembered, and with that memory he was almost ready to forgive her for whatever influence she had had in Wally's taking the R-47 in the first place. Cele was beautiful but Maea was warm, with a human, living warmth.

"Answer some questions for me," he said, in a gentler tone of voice.

"Of course," she said, coming farther into the room. "What about?"

"Your field of temporal sociology. When you make these forecasts of changes that will be caused in the social patterns and culture of a community because of some planned physical or technological change, how accurate are you?"

"Good, within limits," she said. "We can quite accurately identify general trends and project them. Of course, there's no way in the world anyone can imagine what hasn't yet been imagined, invented, or created. An unforeseeable technological improvement, a chemical or medical discovery—anything like that can throw us way off in our picture of how things will be."

"All right," he said. "Give me some examples of how these forecasts have been badly thrown off by discoveries in the last fifteen years."

"Well . . . as a matter of fact," she said, "I can't remember any such discoveries in the last fifteen years. Come to think of it, there hasn't been anything to throw off a modern projection. But of course life's been better for the average person—physically, I mean—and there hasn't been the need to go searching for great new developments in any field."

"Yes. No. Stasis," he said abruptly, his speech unable to keep up with the rush of his thoughts. "Development's been ceasing as culture trended toward perfect balance. The whole structure of society's been altered by a constant drive to even up challenge with response, the response of the EC bureaucracy. It's both a symptom and a result— a result of an attempt to create paradise now, right now, in the present."

"People have always tried to create paradise for themselves," she said, staring fascinated at him.

"Not in their own time. In any one individual's time, all he or she can do is lay the groundwork. The next generation comes along and alters the groundwork to suit themselves. So the building never gets finished. That's healthy. That's the way it was. But now there's no chipping away at foundations laid by the previous generation. We're building the fourth and fifth story on our grandparents' foundations."

"The EC," said Maea, "would probably say that at least our four or five stories are an improvement to always working on the basement. And maybe they've got an argument, but—"

"No. Wrong," he said. "Paradise is perfection. The building going on now is construction on an imperfect base. See the bad things—duels, dolphin-shark fights, hidden files—signs showing the building's out of true. Gets worse as it grows. Finally it'll go smash out of its own mistakes." The excitement or R-Master cerebration was kindling in him, still.

"The Mogows have known that for some time now," she said.

"No. Felt it, thought it, but didn't know it. I *know* it—now. I could draw you a chart if I had two years to draw it in. But I don't. It doesn't matter anyway. . . . You see what I'm driving at?"

"No," she said.

He had gone back once more to pacing up and down the room.

"Imperfection means faults. Faults mean points of weakness. That's what we have to do. How do you fight a bureaucratic system?"

"Expose it?" said Maea.

"Expose what? You can expose the bureaucrats, if you can show what they did they shouldn't have done. But a system? No. A system—a bureaucracy—is nonphysical. Weapons won't work against it. Riots won't work against it. Even laws won't work. It's a thought, a way of thinking. Even a bloodbath—if you killed off all the bureaucrats, they'd start to appear again the next generation as some people slid back into the same old pattern. The only thing that smashes one pattern is a new pattern."

"What new pattern?"

He shook his head and stopped walking. Suddenly he felt drained to the point of exhaustion. He leaned against a wall with one hand and looked at her.

"You want too much," he said, half to himself. "Too much, too soon. I've got to work it out some more. . . ."

He ran down. The headwaters of that furious spate of thought that had been tapped in him were now draining away into the well of an exhaustion deeper than he had ever encountered before.

"I'd better lie down," he said, as much to himself as Maea. He started toward the door.

She came close to him.

"Do you need help?" she asked.

"No," he said. "I can make it."

She did not touch him. But she followed along as he made his way to the door of his bedroom and into it. He fell back at last onto the grav float of his bed.

"Lots to do," he said. "I'll have to get back to work soon. But right now, a little nap—"

He was on his way to sleep before he finished the sentence. Still, somehow he had the impression that Maea sat down silently by the bed, to wait and watch. . . .

He came to, suddenly. Beyond the windows of his bedroom, it was evening. Maea was gone, but Rico was standing over him.

"Sorry, Mr. Ho," said Rico. "I didn't mean to wake you."

"That's all right," said Et. "I shouldn't be asleep anyway." He felt strangely good, almost abnormally free of his usual small discomforts. It was as if his torrent of thought had washed them clean away. He sat up on the edge of the bed.

"What time is it?"

"A little after eight in the evening," said Rico.

Et got to his feet.

"I'd better eat something," he said. "If you didn't want me up, what brought you here?"

"I was hoping to find you already awake," Rico said. "I've been able to pick up some more information, though

I don't know how useful it'll be. For one thing, there's a name for those files, after all. The symbol for them—".

He took a stylus and writing surface from his pocket and marked a couple of glowing swirls upon it, then passed the surface to Et. What he had drawn was o–o.

"In speaking," said Rico, "It's referred to as zero-zero."

"Cancel out," said Et, gazing at the symbol.

"Pardon me?" Rico frowned at him.

"Nothing," said Et. "That symbol just happens to fit something I was thinking about earlier. I got off on a sort of mental binge, did Maea tell you?"

"Yes," said Rico. "Dr. Carwell tells us it was to be expected. Dr. Hoskides says it's a dangerous state to get into without protective drugs."

"I'll bet that's what Hoskides says," said Et, but the memory of what it had been like came back to him. "There may be something in what he's talking about—only not just what he thinks. Never mind that now, though. You wanted to know how we were going to get at these zero-zero files."

"You found a way?"

Et laughed.

"There's dozens of ways," he said. "But the simplest is to have this museum employee, who also works for the EC, go down and bring them up for us."

Rico looked doubtful.

"I should think a man like that would be electronically and chemically protected against physical coercion or anything psychological or technological."

"He can't be booby-trapped against doing his job, however," said Et. "The weakest point in the protections set up around those zero-zero files is the pattern of authority to which the one man with access to them responds. We only need to forge an order for him to look up the files we want."

"An order can be forged, of course," said Rico, "although I'd imagine he'd also need voice authority from some superior; we'd have to fake that too. But getting at the files like that would simply let the EC know what we're after and probably give them enough evidence to trace the whole business back here."

"Not necessarily," said Et.

"How would you avoid it?" Rico asked.

Et shook his head.

"That requires a little working out. But it won't be any trouble." He looked at Rico. "Establishing the particular principle behind the action we need was the important part. In this case, we now know what we want and how we're going to get it. Once those two things are determined, it's merely a matter of identifying all the inherent liabilities to the chosen action and taking steps to counter each one specifically—"

He broke off.

"But you'll have already identified these liabilities, yourself, haven't you?" he said to Rico.

"No," said Rico. "I'm afraid I haven't."

Et nodded slowly.

"Malone was right," he said. "The only way I can tell what the R-47 has done to me is when I run into something which seems plain and simple to me but not to others. But I give you my word, Rico, the details I'm talking about are things I can work out quite easily. You'll just have to trust me."

13

One week after his revival, Wally's body was clearly as far back along the road to life as it was going to go. In essence, it was not Wally at all but a flesh-and-blood automaton, something like a catatonic. The body tended to hold any position in which it was put, but only until it became tired. Then it tumbled to the ground. The eyes were open but unfocusing. The jaws chewed automatically when food was put between the lips. Forcing himself, Et went to see the empty shell—so like his own body—that had once been his brother.

"Try not to let it disturb you," said Carwell, standing beside Et at the foot of the grav-float bed on which Wally lay. He put his large hand gently on Et's shoulder. "There may be some vestiges of a mind left, but the essential part of the brother you knew isn't here at all. What's here doesn't even have any consciousness of existence. Watch."

He stepped away from Et, up to the side of the bed,

and took a small pencil probe from the pocket of his jacket.

"As a body," Carwell said, "it's got perfect nervous responses. But look."

He brought the point of the pencil probe close to the skin on the back of Wally's left hand, which lay laxly beside his body. A tiny spark leaped to bridge the last few millimeters of distance between probe point and skin. But Wally remained motionless, and his face showed nothing.

"See?" said Carwell. "Perfect physically, but from a practical point of view there's almost perfect anesthesia. Skin flinch, which is a reflex, is the only acknowledgment we get. Your brother's body shows an anesthesia stemming from a lack of mental response, not from any failure of the sensory network. Neither comfort nor discomfort, as we know them, exist for this body. There's no consciousness to record them."

He came back to stand facing Et.

"Believe me," he said gently, "this is not your brother."

Et laughed harshly, unable to look away from the figure on the bed.

"According to legend," he said. "They tied the dying Cid on his horse, and he rode out of Valencia to defeat the Almoravids as a dead man. So Wally's body can be used to help destroy the people who cost him his intelligence and then his life."

"Cid?" Carwell stared at him.

"An eleventh-century Spaniard. The most famous of the medieval Spanish captains." Et turned away from the bed. "His real name was Rodrigo Díaz de Vivar. 'Cid' is from the Arabic word *sid*. It means 'lord.' "

They went out. In the room outside were two men in white jumper suits, and around them were various pieces of equipment looking somewhat like the equipment in a gym or a weight-training room. As Et and Carwell nodded at them and went past, out a farther door, the floor of the room gave softly and resiliently under Et's feet.

"They're Mogows, I suppose?" Et asked Carwell as the second door closed behind them and they stepped onto green lawn.

"Mogows we can trust," said Carwell. "More than that, they're good therapists, good at their profession. You needn't have any doubts that they'll handle"—he hesitated—"Wally, as gently as you'd handle him yourself."

Et nodded.

"All right," he said. "I believe you. After looking at Wally just now, though, and remembering all that old business about animal training, it's a little hard for me to warm up to them."

"You're an R-Master," said Carwell. "You shouldn't be affected by old stories."

"I don't know how old they are," Et said, remembering the dueling gym and the tank holding the sharks and dolphins. "What do you want to bet that somewhere in this world some poor damned parrot is reciting the Gettysburg Address or some chimp is playing a whole ensemble of tunes on a flute or a recorder with a special mouthpiece?"

"If there are," said Carwell, "the people who trained them are either already under arrest for the regulations they've broken or about to be. Response therapy may have had its inspiration in training animals, small step by small step, to do a whole complicated chain of actions. But it's become a medical means to help people, humans suffering from a learning inability because of accidental or genetic mental deficiency. It's not a toy in the right hands, Et, it's a tool."

"Morgan," said Et, looking sideways at him as they walked along. "What does 'therapy' mean?"

Carwell was silent.

"So you see," said Et, "we aren't retraining Wally so he can live a fuller life. Because there's no life for him to live at all. We're animal-training him to do a set of tricks that'll fool people into thinking he's me. Remember, doctor? That's the instruction I gave you after Wally was revived. Where's the therapy in that?"

Carwell still said nothing. Only his heavy shoulders hunched a little more. He was like some heavy wounded bear, shambling along, and suddenly Et's pain and disgust turned inward on himself. This time it was he who put his hand on the other's shoulder. He halted Carwell and turned the man to face him.

"Damn it, Morgan, don't listen to me!" he said. "You know I'm just taking out on you what I ought to be taking out on myself. It was my idea to make a living marionette out of Wally, not yours. I know you're a medical man, with an oath to relieve suffering, not cause it; and here I force you into this business with Wally, then throw your oath in your face. I didn't use to be like that. But that's the way I am now. So pay no attention to me when I talk like that."

"No, no," said Carwell, shaking his head. "It's all right. I can't wash my hands. Nobody can."

He turned and lumbered away up the slope of the lawn toward another part of the house. Et watched him go and then went off to find his own mental distraction in the chesslike problem of examining all the possible dangers in their projected scheme to give a forged order to the custodian of the o–o files.

But in spite of himself, during the next two weeks

while Rico and Maea were arranging for the production of the actual false order, through a variety of personal connections between Mogows and EC employees, Et found himself going back to watch the response-training therapists at work with Wally. To someone who knew nothing about the history and scope of this work, the results could hardly have seemed less than magical. Even to Et, what was accomplished was startling.

The principle of response therapy, or training, was extremely simple. It was to break down a complex physical action into a series of very simple actions and teach these simple actions one at a time to a subject. By this means a sequence of movements was gradually built up that became the complex action. The key to its success was the practice of rewarding the subject in training for any movement, even a random one, in the proper direction, so that an association between the correct movements and pleasure was achieved. As Et had said, the principle had first been used by animal trainers, usually in circuses, to produce such performances as a chicken pecking out a tune on a small piano or a dog stealing a wallet from the pocket of a clown and then hiding it in a series of different places as the clown proceeded to search for it.

The great virtue of the training technique from a show-business principle was that its use could produce acts by animals that appeared to have human thought and intelligence behind them. Its virtue as a medical therapy—when the principle was adapted to that use, later on—was that it could be used to teach people with crippling mental deficiencies to perform complicated actions necessary to their participation in the society of the normally intelligent. It had been used, for example, to teach the mentally deprived to feed and dress themselves, to operate simple machinery, and, within certain limitations, to acquire the rudiments of normal adult behavior.

Seventy or eighty years of development, however, had brought it almost to the level of a fine art. In Wally's case, starting with a body essentially capable of nothing more than reflex movement, the response therapists began by working to develop what were referred to as "initiating actions." Since the one base on which they had to build in what had been Wally was the feeding reflex, they set to work to build a movement by which a small piece of candy, put in his hand, would be carried by that hand to his mouth. In this case, the reward of the bit of good-tasting food on Wally's palate was reinforced by a momentary mild stimulation beamed directly from a control cap into the pleasure center of Wally's brain.

From getting Wally to carry a morsel of something eatable to his mouth with a single arm movement, the therapists progressed to teaching him first to grasp and then to reach out and pick up the morsel. By the end of the sixth day they had him sitting up in order to reach out and pick up the reward, and from then on progress was rapid.

By the end of the second week, what the therapists called "muscle pleasure" had entered the situation. This was a turn-of-the-century discovery in response therapy, something particularly useful in the case of training humans and the higher anthropoids. It had been discovered that in most warm-blooded mammals there was a distinct, associative pleasure in physical exertion. This had been recognized since time immemorial in the instances of children at play and athletes, both amateur and professional, engaging in physical sports. But it extended beyond that, throughout the animal kingdom as well, exemplified by horses too long confined in a barn who could not be kept from running and by trained sled dogs who would continue to try to run along beside a team from which they had been cut loose, because they were no longer able to pull properly.

With the awakening of muscle pleasure in the body that had been Wally's, the therapists were able gradually to reduce and finally to abandon the dangerously addictive activity of reward by stimulation of the brain's pleasure center. Meanwhile Wally was now able to rise from his bed in the morning, to dress himself in a simple one-piece coverall, and even to walk around the grounds with one of the therapists in attendance.

For all this, there was still no consciousness behind the eyes of the perambulating figure. Meeting Wally one morning out in the grounds, Et had made the mistake of looking directly into those eyes; after that he could not bring himself to face Wally directly again.

Meanwhile, he completed his plan for getting at the o–o files. By the end of the second week, he and Rico put themselves in the hands of Cye Morecky, a Mogow who had been brought to the island a few days before with the ultimate purpose of working on Wally. Beginning at 3 A.M. one morning and working for two hours, Morecky, using removable skin parts and other stage tools, changed the two of them so that in the end Et and Rico looked not only unlike themselves but enough like each other so that the resemblance would disturb the memory of anyone trying to identify them from recollection alone. They went out, took their atmosphere ship to Miami, and there boarded a commercial ship for New York.

Two hours later, they were pressing the annunciator at the office door of the museum employee who had access to the o–o files.

He opened the door. He was a man past middle age but vigorous-looking in spite of a face folded in deep wrinkles.

"What do you want?" he said. "This isn't part of the public section of the museum—"

"We come from Vienna," said Rico.

"Ah," said the other, stepping back from the door to let them in and then closing it behind them. "Anyone from Vienna is specially welcome. Who are you?"

"I don't think we need to identify ourselves, Mr. Tolicky," Rico said, speaking through a throat filter that altered his voice. "We've given the password; you've given the countersign. We've got something to give you here."

He produced a heavy sealed envelope.

"These are to be copied below and the originals returned to us," said Rico.

"Oh?" said Tolicky. He spoke into the phone on his wrist. "Code nine thousand nine—"

His voice broke off. As he had been speaking, he had been ripping open the envelope. When it came unsealed a little puff of almost invisible vapor shot up in his face. He stopped moving and stood with the torn envelope still in his hands, like someone lost in thought.

Hastily, Et reached out, caught up the old man's wrist, and shut off the phone connection. Taking a small button attached to a short length of what looked like fine wire, he touched the end of the wire to the bone behind Tolicky's ear and spoke. His voice came out through a throat filter, altered and deepened to sound like the voice Tolicky was expecting to hear from the phone.

"*Tolicky? This is Sauvonne. Here are your instructions. Take the envelope contents down for copying as you've been told. This is an order.*"

Et put the button with its wire back out of sight inside his jacket, palmed a miniature vid-transceiver, and hooked it to the shoulder of Tolicky's jacket. Rico was watching his own wrist chronometer. On its tiny screen, a view of the room from the vid-transceiver appeared. At exactly forty seconds after the puff of vapor had escaped from the envelope, Tolicky stirred, blinked, and turned without a word to the wall behind him. At a touch of his hand, the wall slid aside to reveal an old-fashioned vault entrance large enough to walk into. Tolicky put his right thumb into the lock hole and said, "Tolicky. Entering."

The vault opened. The old man went in, and the door closed behind him. Et and Rico followed his movements on the screen of Rico's chronometer. For a second or two the vault seemed to tremble around him; then the door to it opened once more of its own accord, and he stepped out—now seventy meters below his office.

The room Tolicky entered was small and starkly lighted. Along one wall were a row of file cabinets with innumerable little drawers ranked in them. Tolicky paused and drew from the envelope a thick sheaf of imperishable plastic paper bound with metal clamps into a solid unit and topped with an order form several pages in length. Tolicky scanned the form and drew in a hissing breath. On the last page, the signature on the order held his attention for a second.

He turned to a grav-float table surface against the far wall that had what seemed to be a ground glass screen set in it. He spread out the last sheet of the order holding the signature face down on the ground glass and waited for a second.

At the end of that time a word suddenly glowed to life

on the ground glass above the sheet: *Forgery*.

Tolicky chuckled. He put the order and the clamped bundle of sheets back into the envelope and took the vault elevator back up to his office. There he handed them back to Rico. Brushing against him, Et retrieved the tiny vid-transceiver.

"You made the copies?" Rico asked.

"Oh, yes," said Tolicky, almost chuckling again. "I made them. Good day, gentlemen."

They turned toward the door. As they were going out, Tolicky spoke unexpectedly behind them.

"What are you? Auditor Corps men?"

Rico and Et jerked about.

"Certainly not," said Rico. "What makes you think that?"

"Oh, nothing . . . nothing," said Tolicky cheerfully, with a wave of his hand. "Just every so often, one of the other sections decides they'd like to run a little test on me, that's all."

They went on out. As they closed the door behind them, they could hear Tolicky laughing.

"We'd better move fast," Et said, in his altered voice. They went swiftly to the nearest slideramp, up to the street, and took an automated cab to the Harbor Terminal. An hour later by commercial atmosphere ship saw them back in Miami, and thirty minutes after that they were back at a table in a laboratory room on the island, stripping the envelope from its contents.

Et let the order flutter unheeded to the floor. But with great care he pried off the metal clamps. With these no longer holding the apparent sheaf of papers together, the top half inch of them came off like a box lid. Inside was a space packed with what seemed to be tiny crystals hardly bigger than grains of sand.

"Careful," said Rico. "Don't breathe on them."

He slid the now-exposed mass of crystals into an aperture in a large metal device on the table to their right and sealed the opening behind it.

"Now," he said, with something that was almost a sigh of relief. "The rest of the process is automatic."

"You didn't explain to me," said Et, "how this works."

"You're right, I didn't. I'm sorry, Mr. Ho," said Rico. "The crystals are from one of the many research laboratories funded by the EC. So far they haven't been released for commercial use. They're grown completely within a grav field, under no particular stress lines. However, once they're removed from the protection of the grav field enclosing them—as they were when the cover was taken off their package in the secret file room—they immediately develop stress lines in response not only to gravitational pull but to mass objects within a radius of some twelve meters of area surrounding them."

"Clever of them," said Et. "How does that help us?"

"These stress lines can be interpreted by computer," said Rico. "It's essentially the same process as when they use a computer to clean up and sharpen one of the photographs of Mars or Pluto or any other stellar body. That interpretation of the crystals we have here should give us a complete picture, not only of the files in the basement but of all the information in the files."

"Good enough," said Et. "I'm going to get out of this makeup now."

He went off to do so. When he came back, Rico—still in his own makeup—was poring over a readout on a screen attached to the machine in which he had put the crystals. The secretary looked up, pleased, as Et came in.

"We got everything," he said. "Everything for five meters in each direction, including the rock structure around the sub-basement and a full set of details on Tolicky's insides. Of course, it's going to take a few days to sort out the information we're after. Luckily, the files are set up according to a system, or we'd have to go through the equivalent of a large library of information to get what we want."

"How soon?" Et asked.

"How soon will we have what we want? A day or so."

"Good," said Et. "Call me if I can be of any help. I think I'm going to have to lie down for a bit."

He went back to his own room. He had been geared up again during the actual visit to the museum and had forgotten all his small discomforts, but now these were back, compounded by the deep weariness that always followed excitement. He dropped off into a dreamless sleep, from which he was roused by the sound of his bedside phone.

He rolled over on one elbow in the darkened room and punched the *on* stud. The screen surface of the phone lit up with the image of Rico, at last out of makeup.

"What is it?" asked Et thickly.

"Cele Partner," said Rico. "Reverberations from our little visit to the museum are beginning, evidently. Patrick St. Onge called just about half an hour ago to see how you'd recovered from your cold—but pretty plainly wanting to find out if you'd left the island. I told him you were over being sick but still weak. Now Miss Partner wants to talk to you."

"We still don't know for sure that she's connected with the EC," said Et.

"I'll make you a small bet that I find a dossier on her in the zero-zero files and proof she's connected with St Onge and the auditors," answered Rico.

"All right, put her on," said Et.

Rico's face dissolved on the screen and Cele's face formed.

"Et?" she said. "Et, are you there? I can't see you."

"Just a minute," he said.

He turned on a bedside light. From the screen he could see her examining his appearance closely.

"You're still sick, then?" she asked.

"Not really," said Et. "Just a little wobbly."

"What a shame! I was going to suggest we might get together in New Orleans this evening. I had some business over here, and I'm on your time schedule."

"Any time I can't make it to New Orleans from here, I'm in bad shape," said Et.

"How about eight o'clock, *this* time?"

"Eight will be fine. Eight by yours."

"I'll be looking forward to it. Good evening."

"Evening."

They broke connection. Et lay where he was for a moment, on one elbow propped up on his bed. Then he called Rico.

"Did you listen in?" he asked the secretary.

"No, Mr. Ho. Should I, from now on?"

"Yes . . . no. No, on second thought. But you'll be glad to hear, if you're right about Cele, they're beginning to take the bait. I'm to have dinner with her in New Orleans at eight. I'll try to bring her back here afterward to see Wally. Better get a mustache on him."

"He'll be ready, Mr. Ho."

14

Flying from the island to New Orleans in his private atmosphere ship, Et had time to wonder if he was doing the right thing. It was not the first time he had so wondered, since the day Garranto had said that whatever had been given Wally in place of R-47 had directly caused Wally's mental disintegration and death and Et had made his decision to smash the system that had brought about those things. Once more, he came to the simple conclusion that he had no alternative to his present course of action.

He was the only one who could be trusted to see the situation in its entirety. No one but an R-Master could hold the complete picture of it in his mind; the only other R-Master in this matter was Malone, who was unpredictable. That meant all the other people involved—Rico, Carwell, Maea—must be brought to act on a portion of the full facts, as if that portion was the whole story. Cele and St. Onge offered the least problems, because all Et had to do with those two was sell them a bill of goods. Et had no doubt that Rico was right, in that St. Onge had been set, with Cele as his assistant, to keep a special watch over the newest R-Master. Rico himself would need to know the most and must therefore be the one whom Et had to trust the most, but Et felt a strange faith in the smaller man that was unusually serene. He had better be right about that, however, because it would be Rico and Malone who would have to operate on their own, once Et had done his part and sent the Section Chiefs of the Earth Council on the way to their own destruction.

Meanwhile, the first step was Cele. She knew him to be many times her mental equal now that the R-47 was in him, but she would be counting on that part of him that was unchanged, the emotional male part, as an arena in which she could win any encounter. At that—a little touch of uneasiness troubled the surface of his mind for a second —she might be right. He was, after all, still only human, only a man.

They went to dinner that evening in New Orleans at a historic old restaurant called Brennan's. Just as it had been on the evening of his first visit to Malone in San Diego, the weather was unseasonably cool. They sat at a small round table with spidery ironwork legs, exposed to the stars in a courtyard with old-fashioned radiant heaters set in the high stone walls surrounding them, so that they were half-warmed, half-chilled as they sipped their drinks.

After the drinks, they went inside the weather shield to the terrace of the restaurant proper. There were no live waiters as there had been once, half a century and more ago; but a live maître d' circulated among the tables in white tie and tails, and the seafood was memorable.

Cele peered at him in the candlelight as they sat with coffee and green chartreuse after the meal.

"You do look tired," she said.

"Yes," said Et.

For indeed he did. The Mogow makeup expert who had prepared him and Rico for the visit to the museum had made some slight changes in his appearance in the few minutes available tonight before he had left the island. Some sort of liquid injected under his eyes and at their corners had loosened the skin there, and a faintly dark powder had been rubbed into the skin below the eyes as well. Other tiny changes at the corners of his mouth and nose and along his jawline had faintly aged him, so that the difference between the image he presented to the world and the one Wally would present would be marked by something more than the mustache he had mentioned to Rico earlier.

"I'm just worn down a little," Et said now. "It's been kind of a tense time. We revivified my brother."

"Your brother?" said Cele. "Oh, yes, I remember. Did it go all right?"

"Better than that," said Et. "He may come out of it better than he went in. You know, it was R-47 that knocked him down. He had a bad reaction. But now he seems to be coming back with something like his original intelligence."

"How wonderful!"

"Wonderful and then some," said Et. "It's a miracle. Of course the physicians said that a death shock could conceivably do something like this, but the chances were one in millions. But then, long shots sometimes pay off. I'm an example of that."

"Was he a younger or older brother?"

"Three years older. They say we look like twins though."

"Oh?"

He thought he caught a new note of interest in her voice.

"Yes." he said. "Come and see me at my island sometime, and you can decide if it's true for yourself."

"Maybe," she said thoughtfully, "I will."

"Of course"—he leaned a little closer to her—"you could fly back with me tonight, come to think of it. I could take you sailing in the *Sarah*."

"The *Sarah*?"

"My boat," he said. "The one I had before I took the R-47. It's not a toy I picked up since; it's an oceangoing sloop. It'll be a good night for sailing tonight, at the island. Almost a full moon."

Cele laughed and shook her head.

"I'm not dressed for getting all windblown in a sailboat," she said. "I'm not really in the mood for it, either. But I might take a look at your island anyway."

"Then let's go."

They flew back in Et's atmosphere ship. Once they were landed, Et led her on a general tour of the island, avoiding the route that would take them to Wally's quarters directly. It was necessary to give Rico, Carwell, and the others plenty of time to have Wally ready for Cele to see. Also, he admitted to himself, it was pleasant strolling around in the dark. The moon was almost full, as he had said, and the Caribbean night was soft. For a little while it was almost the way it had always been with him, in the days before Wally took the R-47 and he himself followed in Wally's footsteps.

They came at last to the docks, toward which he had been aiming all along. But when they came down along the wooden surface, hollow-sounding under their feet, there was a light in the cabin of the *Sarah;* and through a side porthole of the cabin, when they got a little closer, Et saw the heads of Al and Maea, laughing together at something.

"Why are you stopping?" Cele asked. "Isn't your boat here after all?"

"It's here," Et said grimly. "But I'd forgotten something. I gave the boat to somebody else."

He turned and led the way back up the dock to the soft turf and on up to the house, directly to Wally's quarters. Carwell was waiting for them as they came up to the entrance of the wing.

"Who's that?" Carwell said, moving toward them in the gloom. "Oh, Mr. Ho. Were you going to look in on your brother?"

"Yes," said Et. Somehow, he had expected Carwell to be a poor actor, just as he would have expected him to be a poor liar. But the big man surprised him. Carwell's words sounded more natural than Et's own planned response.

"Cele, this is Dr. Morgan Carwell, my personal physician—and my brother's," said Et. "Dr. Carwell, Miss Cele Partner."

Cele and Carwell murmured acknowledgments of the introduction.

"Wallace is asleep. He's had quite a day," Carwell said. "If you don't mind, Mr. Ho, I'd prefer that he wasn't disturbed, now that he's sleeping. These first few weeks are crucial, particularly in a case like this where he's regaining the mental acuity he lost earlier. We want to give him every chance to rebound as far as he can."

"Perhaps," said Et, "Miss Partner could just look through the observation window from the therapy room?"

"Of course," said Carwell. "Let me lead the way."

He took them in through the wing, to the therapy room, and across its padded floor to the observation window that gave a view of Wally's bedroom.

"I could turn on the lights without disturbing him," Carwell said to Cele. "One-way glass. But with the glare of light on this side you wouldn't be able to see him so well in the dark. If I leave the lights off here, the night light in there is just enough . . ."

"I see," said Cele, looking through the glass. Her voice was thoughtful. "You're right, Et; he does look a lot like you."

"That's what people say," said Et.

Wally lay on his side, in the position they had taught him, rather than flat on his back as he had on first being revived. The night light showed his unlined face clearly against the pillow, the mustache a black smudge on his upper lip.

"Yes," murmured Cele, gazing at him, "a remarkable resemblance . . ."

She turned abruptly from the window.

"Well, Et," she said, suddenly energetic, "what else haven't you shown me on this island of yours?"

"You've seen it all outdoors," Et said. "How about indoors?"

"Of course. You've got a terrace somewhere, out under the stars, haven't you, where we can sit and have a drink? Come along and have a drink with us, Dr. Carwell, won't you?"

She put a hand on Carwell's thick arm.

"I'd enjoy it," he told her.

"Good—Morgan," she said. "And you can tell me all about Et's brother. It fascinates me. Someone brought back from a terminal situation in better shape than he went into it."

They went to the terrace. Et had thought that one drink would probably be the end of it, but Cele turned out to be as fascinated with Wally's revival as she had said. She kept Carwell in conversation about Wally until Et's head began to spin achingly from fatigue plus his own new vulnerability to liquor and late hours. Finally he excused himself and went to bed, leaving them still talking.

He dreamed, but of Maea. He woke and lay in the darkness, remembering the sight of her laughing with Al on the boat, before he finally rolled over on his other side and got to sleep without dreams.

The next morning, Cele was gone. That evening, after dinner, Rico called Et down to the room where he had been reconstructing the information obtained by the crystals from the o–o files.

"I've got it," Rico said, "Everything you asked me to find out." There were dark smudges under his eyes, the shadows of fatigue and strain.

"Good," said Et. "First, what about Cele Partner?"

Rico punched buttons below a viewscreen, and a paragraph of close print leaped to life on its gray surface.

"There's her dossier," said Rico.

Et looked. It was not a short dossier. Cele, he learned, had been born with the name of Maria Van Pelt, in Brussels, Belgium. She had evidently deduced for herself the existence and power of what Rico called the bureaucracy and set out to join it for her own benefit. She had taken a clerical job with one of the EC subsidiaries in Rangoon and proved her worth to the Accounting Section by uncovering a number of instances there of regulations being broken. She had attracted the attention of St. Onge and since that time had been on special duty, responsible only to him.

"Good enough," said Et. "With any luck, she'll have taken the bait; she'll be telling St. Onge right now how convenient it'd be to have Wally in my place. What've they got on Lee Malone?"

Rico punched buttons again. The dossier this time was even longer. They had to blow it up to make it readable and fill the screen with several successive sections of it.

"Now that's hitting pay dirt," said Et.

"I thought you'd say so," Rico answered. "Note that Master Malone is recorded as having been treated not with R-47 but something called R-48k. Also, there's no mention of the laboratory in his basement. If the EC knew about it, mention of it would certainly be there."

"Those are two things I was reasonably sure about anyway," said Et. "What pleases me more is that they've taken him at his own image; they evidently believe he's nothing but a talker, with no real revolutionist fire in him."

"Can we be sure that isn't actually all he is?" Rico looked sidelong at Et.

"I'm sure," said Et. "A man who was a talker rather than an actor wouldn't have worked that long, that hard, and kept the secret of his laboratory that well. No, Malone is safe for the moment—and he ought to be able to stay safe at least while he makes enough of the improved R-47 for our use. You did find information here about the improved version of the R-47?"

"Yes. Here."

Rico punched buttons again. The image that formed on a screen looked to Et like nothing so much as a page from a chemistry textbook.

"Can Malone follow that?"

"If he can't," said Rico, "I can. The chemistry at this point is simple enough. Actually what I'm showing you is the end result, essential information on a long process of research and development of the drug we know as R-47. This variation is called R-50."

"There's always the chance, though," said Et, "that it isn't the actual, final, successful variant. They must have found that and then thrown away the information as too dangerous."

"No," said Rico. "If I know anything, I know the bureaucratic mind. It never throws anything away. It's exactly in character with whatever eighteen Section Chiefs sit on the EC Council at any one time, to make sure that R-47 was refined to the ultimate point and then to bury the results here, where they'd never be used. Give me Malone's equipment and experience, and I'll produce the actual drug for you."

"All right, I'll take your word for it," said Et. "Now let's look at some more dossiers. Yours, to begin with."

Without a word, Rico punched buttons. The dossier that appeared on the screen was lengthy and remarkable in the skills it attributed to Rico, but there was no hint that he was considered anything but utterly loyal to the EC.

"All right," said Et. "Wally."

Wally had a very brief biographical section, followed by the note: *possible active member of Mogow.* Appended to this was a note concerning his revivification.

"Maea," said Et.

Maea's bio was similarly brief and had the same added note that possibly she was an active Mogow member.

"Carwell." But Carwell was not in the o–o files.

"Try me," Et said.

His own entry was hardly longer than those of Wally

and Maea. His becoming an R-Master was mentioned, as were his connections with possible Mogows such as Maea and Wally. There was a note that, over Medical objection, Patrick St. Onge had been assigned to surveillance of him.

"Why '*over Medical objection*'?" Et asked. "And why the capital M?"

"The different Section Chiefs of the Council are always feuding," Rico said. "In particular, Wilson of Accounting and Saya Sorenson of Medical are at each other's throats, because they've come to be heads of the two sections of the EC with the most members in them. There was probably some political reason for Saya to object to you being placed under surveillance. Chances are it had nothing to do with you personally."

"No?" said Et. "I'd guess it had a great deal to do with me personally. Let's see the entry on Dr. Garranto y Vega."

"Garranto?" Rico looked surprised. "Why would he be in the zero-zero files? I don't think we'll find an entry on him."

"Try," said Et.

Rico tried, and an entry was found. It was brief. Dr. Garranto was noted as an individualist who had the bad habit of ignoring Medical Section regulations. He had been secretly reprimanded for a particular breach of regulations some four years before.

"I don't understand," said Rico, looking from the entry to Et.

"I see a connection," Et said. "Tell me, what besides the size of the membership in their sections would bring Medical and Accounting into conflict in the EC?"

"Accounting contains the Auditor Corps, the police arm of the EC," said Rico. "Medical doesn't like its physicians hassled by Field Examiners; it thinks professional people should be above that. Of course, all this is very polite, and kept to arguments in the Economic Council. No one in top position in the EC's going to rock the boat."

"Perhaps," said Et. "I'd been suspecting that Medical and Accounting weren't together on everything, and I rather suspected what we found out about Dr. Garranto."

"Then maybe you'd tell me what that has to do with what we're trying to do," said Rico. "We're just trying to get the R-50 drug loose and out to people, aren't we?"

"Not exactly," said Et. "We're trying to get R-50 loose and out to people—but under conditions where it'll do some good."

"I've been taking that particular qualification of yours for granted," said Rico.

"You shouldn't," retorted Et. "What if we got the drug into production and some new R-Masters made, only to have it and them suddenly swept up by the EC and quietly eliminated? What you tell me about Medical and Accounting backs up the way the whole picture's been fitting together. If the feud between even two EC sections is serious enough, we can't trust these oo files completely."

"But these files are the one thing none of the Section Chiefs would monkey with," began Rico.

"It wouldn't take monkeying with the files themselves," said Et. "But never mind that now. You'd better get the R-50 information to Malone as quickly as possible. Take it yourself. When you reach him, help him pack up his necessary lab equipment and clear out of that home of his; then have him use his more militant Mogow connections for hiding places and keep on the move. You understand?"

Rico looked at him for a moment, as if about to speak, and then apparently changed his mind. He nodded.

"Take Al with you," Et said. "Leave him with Malone. I particularly don't want the EC getting their hands on Al. Meanwhile, I take it Wally's been brought along by the response therapists to where he can put on a fair imitation of me as long as he doesn't have to talk to anyone?"

"Yes," said Rico.

"When I give you the word, it'll be up to you to set up Wally to face the Section Chiefs, without anyone else knowing about it. You're sure you can handle that without trouble?"

"Mr. Ho," said Rico. "I'm not going to let that remark irritate me. I know you're suffering your usual discomforts, and you're under pressure as well."

Et sagged a little.

"All right," he said. He wiped his hand across his forehead and it came away wet. "I'm sorry. Forgive me. I trust you, Rico, of course. We have to trust each other. Tell me again, though. You're sure nothing can ordinarily be smuggled into a meeting of the EC Section Chiefs?"

"Believe me, it can't," said Rico. "Everyone coming in is searched to the skin."

"All right. Then I'll get going," said Et. "I—Wally, that is—had better leave the island tonight. Have that makeup man come to my room and fit me with a fake mustache, will you? I suppose you've already spoken to Al about the boat?"

"Yes," said Rico.

"Good," said Et, opening the door from the room to the outside and the warm island early evening. "In forty-five minutes, the *Sarah* and I will be in open water."

15

Et, in the persona of Wally, sailed the *Sarah* to Fort-de-France and left her there, moored in a public marina on the Madame River. He had Wally's citizen card, to the credit account of which he, as Et, had deposited a healthy amount of units to reinforce the arrears of Wally's own allowance, which had been automatically reactivated on his revival. Therefore, he took a private room on an intercontinental to London and began to wander eastward around the globe, drinking, gambling, scattering credit about—and making it a point to get into arguments and fights wherever he went.

On the third day he was in the Istanbul area, in a pleasure hotel in Galata, sitting in a grav lounge by the huge interior swimming pool of the hotel, when he heard his— or rather, Wally's—name mentioned.

"Wallace Ho?"

Et was half asleep. The strain of appearing to lead the

sort of dissipated life that a physically healthy Wally was supposed to be leading had brought him close to a state of exhaustion, for all that he spent most of his time out of the public eye in sleeping. But the voice that spoke to him was the voice of Cele. He kept his head down and his eyes half closed, however, until she spoke again.

"Aren't you Wallace Ho?"

He looked up and to his right and saw her sitting at a table under a pool umbrella only a few feet away. She was not dressed for swimming, however, but for the street, in skirt and half-blouse. Under the shade of the umbrella she looked as impossibly beautiful as a dream out of the Arabian nights.

"Who're you?" Et said.

"I know your brother—slightly," Cele said. "I passed by his island and stayed to talk to a Dr. Morgan Carwell. I saw you. You were sleeping at the time. But Dr. Carwell told me all about you."

"Very damned interesting," said Et, "but you still haven't told me your name. That was my question— who're *you?*"

"Cele Partner," she said. "Morgan Carwell never mentioned me?"

"He never mentioned anything," said Et.

She laughed, a warm, low-pitched laugh.

"Maybe he was a little jealous," Cele said. "I told him you fascinated me. Someone who'd been brought back not just from the dead but from a bad reaction to R-47. Do you know that you're unique?"

"Being unique doesn't do me any good," said Et. "It's my brother who gets all the advantages—just for being lucky. But then, I never was lucky."

"Aren't you?" said Cele. "I'd have thought you would

be. Now, your brother Et didn't impress me at all."

"Oh?" said Et. "That's a change. Women used to fall all over him. None of them ever fell all over me."

"Maybe they didn't have the sense to appreciate you," said Cele.

He sat up in his chair. "You're serious, aren't you?" he said. "You're actually telling me you get some kind of lift out of me. You've got strange tastes."

"Why don't you join me?" she said.

He got up from his lounge and sat down at her table.

"Actually," she said, "I'd heard you'd left the island. I've been looking for you. I'm glad I finally found you."

They were together for the next five days, an experience that threatened to shake Et loose from most of his certainties. This Cele Partner was entirely different from the one he had met as Etter Ho. The former Cele had been aloof, holding herself at arm's length and seemingly preferring to stay on a pedestal rather than stepping down to common earth with any man. This Cele was just the opposite. The less Et, in his guise as Wally, tried to please her, the more attentive she became to him. There was a fire in her now that he could not have imagined before. In spite of himself—though he was careful to hide the reaction—his own feelings toward her were kindled by it. He was sure enough that he did not love her. But acting as she did, how could he fail to want her?

But what was real about her and what was not? Was the Cele he had first known the true Cele Partner? Or was this present woman the true version? Was what he now saw an act put on at the orders of Patrick St. Onge or someone else? Or had the earlier Cele been acting a part?

Meanwhile, he was moving them eastward to his destination, which was the same gambling area of Hong Kong he had visited before. Once more he gambled, and this time he made sure to lose steadily. The day after they got there, his credit was exhausted and he turned to Cele for units.

For the first time, she refused him something, though the refusal was given sweetly enough. She sat in his lap and ran her fingers through his hair, begging him to understand that she lived almost on a day-to-day basis as far as her GWP allowance was concerned. It was a slightly better allowance than the basic, because she had once written a play that was still being performed, but it was barely enough to keep her going.

He shoved her away, onto the floor.

"You're no good to me," he said and stalked out.

Once beyond the door of the hotel suite, he went down to the main bar and drank for a while, using what little credit remained to him. After a bit, he went to a phone booth. Luckily, communications, like local transportation, were free, a fact he had taken advantage of in the old days when operating the *Sarah* took all of his basic allowance.

After some little delay, the face of Rico looked at him out of the phone screen. Across a satellite communications circuit that was sure to be tapped and recorded by the EC, they exchanged glances.

"I don't want to talk to you!" Et snapped. "Get me that brother of mine. He'd better talk to me, or he'll be sorry he didn't."

"Mr. Ho," said Rico, "Master Ho has asked me to tell you that not only won't he talk to you now, he doesn't want to talk to you at any time in the future; and he also says that it'll do you no good to keep calling, because that decision is final."

"All right," said Et thickly. "You give him a message for me then. He can shut me out all right, if he likes; but he's not going to go on living like a king while I have to scrape along on a basic allowance. He can sit on his island and pretend I don't exist, if he wants, but he's going to have to pay for the privilege. I can be trouble for him. Wait and see if I can't."

"What are you going to do, Wallace?" Rico asked.

"Never mind what I'm going to do. Maybe I've got a friend. Maybe I'm going to have more friends. Maybe things'll start working for me; then he'll wish he hadn't acted so damn high and mighty."

Rico sighed.

"Do you want me to go and tell Master Ho that?" he said. "I don't think it will improve the way he feels toward you at the moment."

"I don't care how he feels," Et said. "He and his feelings can go to hell. All I want is some funds to make life livable. He's got all the credit in the world."

"But he can't use it to give to other people, even to his brother. That's the one thing the Auditor Corps has already told him they won't allow."

"Don't tell me that. He could sneak all the units I want and they'd never know it, let alone complain about it."

"How much do you want?"

"How much can I get?"

"I . . . it's not for me to say, of course," said Rico. Once more his glance met Et's meaningfully. "It would depend on how soon you wanted it. The best estimate I could give you would be that in a week you could have, say, a couple of thousand."

"A week?" said Et. "How about three days from now? How about tomorrow?"

"I'm afraid," said Rico slowly, "that if it had to be to-morrow or even three days from now, it would have to be nothing. It would have to be at least a week. But then you could have two thousand. Three days after that, it might be possible to make it four thousand."

Et nodded.

"Go to hell!" he said and punched off.

He got up and left the phone booth. He did not have to pretend to be half drunk, because the drinks he had had at the bar were affecting him heavily. But despite them, his R-Master mind was able to consider the information he had just gotten. The request for funds had been set up ahead of time with Rico as a code to allow Et to dis-cover what Lee Malone would be able to do in the way of producing doses of R-50. The answer from Rico that it would take a week to produce the first two thousand doses was not encouraging. Even two thousand new R-Masters was a tiny assault force with which to threaten the bureaucratic organization tightly controlling every technological service and every source of supply for a world controlled at a population limit of four billion peo-ple. But judging from Cele's refusal to feed him more credit to gamble with, things were moving to a climax in the game he was playing with her and those behind her.

Well, if they had to make do with two thousand doses, they would have to make do. He went unsteadily back up to the hotel suite he shared with Cele and found her gone. He collapsed on the bed in the bedroom and let his drunken stupor pull him down into heavy sleep.

He was wakened by hotel employees who had roused him in order to evict him. Cele was still missing. He allowed himself to be put out in the street. It was a new day; half a block down the street was a bank where he could draw one more day's worth of his basic allowance. It would not be enough to gain back the hotel suite he had just left but it would be sufficient to feed and house him in a more reasonable hotel.

However, when he got to the bank he discovered that an almost unheard-of thing—a debit—had been charged against his account. The bank had somehow discovered charges of his which, through computer error, had not been placed against his account earlier, and now these charges had to be paid. They amounted to the worth of his basic allowance for the next thirty-nine days.

There was one stage lower than that of someone on minimum basic allowance. That was to become an occupant of the Earth Council Free Shelters—generally, last refuges for people who because of mental or physical deficiencies could not take on even the small responsibility of drawing a daily allowance and using it correctly to maintain themselves. Et looked up the nearest Free Shelter in the local directory and went to it.

He was given a small cubicle of a room and a filling if unremarkable breakfast, in a general dining room where he was surrounded by the incapable, aged, and infirm of both sexes. Breakfast over, he made his way to the Sunset Hut, that same sprawling hotel and casino he had visited shortly after becoming an R-Master.

Inside, Et looked up the Director of Services desk.

"I understand," he said, "that there's a fencing school here at the Hut."

"Yes, sir," said the girl behind the desk. "Wing Forty-four of the hotel, and follow the signs."

Et made his way to Wing Forty-four of the hotel and found, as he had been advised, plaques on the wall pointing the way to *Fencing*. These brought him eventually to what looked like the outer lobby of an athletic club.

"Sir?" said the male attendant behind the desk.

"I heard," said Et, "that a man in need of money could borrow against his body here, if he volunteered for bouts with unbuttoned weapons."

The politeness dropped from the clerk like a discarded mask.

"I'm afraid not," he said coldly. "You've been listening to one of the stories that circulate around the gaming tables."

Et started to turn away.

"However—" said the clerk.

Et turned back.

"However," the other repeated, "we do have gentlemen sometimes willing to sponsor amateurs in bouts with unbuttoned weapons. I could put you on a list. Do you fence at all?"

"In secondary school I did a little with it," said Et.

"All right." The clerk reached under the counter separating them and came up with a sheet of paper and a plastic tab on which was printed a number. "You're Eight-seven-three. Sign this release; then go in to the aid station. Tell them to give you a physical. After that, come back here and wait. Your number tab will give you credit for food and drink while you're waiting."

Et followed the instructions. It was a good three hours after he had been given a cursory going-over by the medical man in the aid station before he heard his number called over the public-address system.

"Number Eight-seven-three," said the bored voice of the announcer, "report to gym Twelve B. Number Eight-seven-three to gym Twelve B immediately."

Et consulted a map of the hotel wing he was in and found his route to Twelve B. When he stepped through the door of its entrance he found himself on a gym floor in a room with a balcony—very much like the one in which he had witnessed the sword fight once before, except that in this case the balcony seats were empty. In fact, there was no one else visible in the room at all, except a man holding a pair of weapons, very like fencing sabers but with sharpened points.

"Are you—" Et was beginning, when the man cut him short.

"Of course not. Here, take one of these. Your sponsor will be in directly."

"Are you the one I'm supposed to fight?" asked Et, taking one of the blades. "Where's the crowd?"

"No, I work here. And there isn't any crowd, just you and your sponsor."

"But if he's sponsoring me to fight someone—"

"Don't be more of a damn fool than you have to be," said the other impatiently. "He's sponsoring you to fight *him*, of course. He's specified no crowd, and as long as he's willing to pay for privacy it makes no difference to us. As far as your own terms with him go, you work those out with him yourself; we don't even want to know about it."

He pushed the other weapon into Et's hands.

"Here, give him this when he shows up. I can't wait here all day."

He went out.

For a long moment, Et stood alone in the room, holding both blades. Then there was the sound of a door opening off to his right. He turned, to see Patrick St. Onge, wearing the type of tight-fitting black suit Et had seen before

on his previous visit to this part of the Sunset Hut. St.
Onge came across the gym floor toward him. At the same
moment there was the noise of another opening door
above, on the balcony. Looking up, Et saw Cele, dressed
in something gauzy and springlike, come down to the edge
of the balcony and lean over.

"Wally," she called. "Here's a gentleman who wants to
meet you. His name's Patrick St. Onge."

Et looked back at St. Onge. The tall man came up to
Et, took one of the blades from him, and stepped back to
salute with it.

"Guard," he said, and he himself fell into guard position.

"Wait a minute," said Et. He looked up at the balcony.
"Cele!"

"I'm afraid I can't do anything more for you right now,
Wally!" called Cele sweetly.

"Guard," said St. Onge again.

Slowly, Et moved his blade up into guard. He felt
unbelievably clumsy while, facing him, St. Onge looked
as if he had been born in the guard position. The other
man's face was expressionless. Only when Et looked at
the auditor's dark eyes closely was he able to make out
something a little eager, a little hungry, in the squinted
lines about them.

"Come, come, let's not waste time," said St. Onge.

He dropped his saber point carelessly to the wooden
floor. Desperately, Et lunged. There was a flash of light
reflected from metal, a ringing, clashing sound as the blades
came together, and Et's weapon was wrenched out of his
grasp. He stood frozen, feeling the sharp point of St.
Onge's blade pricking the skin at the base of his throat.

St. Onge laughed, but without moving his blade. The
point of it stayed poised and ready.

"Do you realize," St. Onge said quietly, "you didn't even set a price on this carcass of yours before you started? Tell me now. What's your body worth—and where should I send the money? To your brother?"

"Damn you!" swore Et. "You can't kill me—just like that!"

"Can't I?" St. Onge laughed, his point still pricking Et's throat. "Why not? You signed a release. An aberrant act, but not an unexpected one. You apparently came out of that revivification from a cryogenic state with an improved intellect but with an emotional instability, Wallace Ho. I'm an auditor, from EC Accounting, and I've had some experience with unstable personalities. Give me one reason not to kill you."

"All right, I'll give you one!" flared Et. "You can use me. The EC can use me, if you want to get rid of that brother of mine!"

"Oh?" St. Onge's eyes flickered suddenly, up to the balcony where Cele was and then back down again to Et. "What makes you think the EC would like to get rid of any R-Master, least of all our latest one?"

"Do I need to tell you?" retorted Et. "I know he'll have been trying to make trouble for you. That's the way he is." Et laughed with what he hoped was the right note of bitterness. "That's life for you. I'm ready to co-operate any way you want. He never would cooperate. And which one of us are you trying to kill off right now? Me! When you'd be ten times better off with me in his place and him dead!"

The point of the unbuttoned saber fell away from its touch against Et's neck.

"Well, well," said St. Onge softly. "So you think you'd make a better R-Master than your brother?"

"I know I would."

There was the sound of feet on steps. Cele descended a stair from the balcony and came up to the two of them.

"Well," said St. Onge, tossing his weapon aside, "maybe you'll have the chance to prove that, Wally. Come along."

There was an unmarked autocar waiting for them outside the Sunset Hut. It took them back to the same hotel and hotel suite from which Et had been evicted the day before. There, St. Onge and Cele waited while Et dressed in fresh clothes and, at St. Onge's orders, shaved off the mustache he had grown to replace the fake one he had originally been wearing.

"All right," said St. Onge, when Et came back into the room. "I'm convinced. You look enough like your brother to pass a casual examination. Now sit down and listen to me."

Et sat.

"Your brother Et," said St. Onge, "avoided normal society most of his life. As a result he managed to grow up without acquiring the almost instinctive understanding of how the world works that all the rest of us have. But I think you understand."

"Try me," said Et.

"I think," said St. Onge, "you, like everyone else, learned a long time ago that there's one price everybody has to pay to have our world the good place it presently is—without wars, without starvation, without plagues, with a good life possible to everyone. In return for all this, there's just one requirement: we all have to live by the regulations. Unless the overwhelming majority lives by the regulations, the system won't work. That's why we crack down on criminals—and that's why you're going to get the chance to take your brother's place."

"You mean," said Et, "if I do step into his shoes I've got to stick by the regulations? Of course I will."

"Don't say it so lightly," said St. Onge. "Because you're going to have to start out by breaking a regulation, at your own risk. You're going to have to be the one to claim to be Etter Ho. All we'll do is help you take your case to the Earth Council. Neither Cele nor myself nor anyone on the Council is going to so much as bend a regulation in its own right for you."

"Well, what good is that?" said Et. "He can prove who he is by fingerprints, eyeprints, and a dozen other things."

"To be sure," said St. Onge, "but we'll make a point of discovering that one of the Ho brothers, aided by someone we haven't yet identified, got into some ultra-secret government files. We guess that their purpose was to switch the master identification files of Wallace and Etter. Since we think the files may have been switched, and since you claim to be Etter, the man now masquerading as Etter must be Wally, the brother Etter managed to have revived from cryogenic suspension. Unfortunately Etter—you, that is—didn't realize that such subjects of cryogenic suspension can suffer brain damage in the process of suspension, with the result that they emerge with criminal inclinations. Apparently this may have happened to your brother Wally, who then got into the files I was talking about and switched them in an effort to gain for himself the perquisites of a R-Master. Understand, none of us know this to be true, but we believe the files may have been switched, and you swear that you are Etter—don't you?"

"Of course," said Et. "But what about lie detector tests, or a dozen other ways of checking—"

"None of these are completely reliable. Under proper

drugs, the truth can be gotten at, of course," said St. Onge, getting to his feet. "But we will assume that the man now masquerading as Etter refuses to take drugs; the regulations protect him in that. There's no way we can force him to take any such thing. On the other hand, you'd be perfectly willing to be questioned under the proper drugs, wouldn't you?"

"Of course," said Et, almost without hesitation.

"Don't worry." St. Onge smiled. "I have great faith that you'll confirm your identity as Etter under any drugs we give you. Just as I have confidence that, faced with this evidence, the EC Section Chiefs will confirm you as the real Etter Ho, R-Master. Of course, once you're reinstated in your proper identity, you'll naturally have no objection to putting yourself under the direction of Dr. Hoskides, Etter Ho's assigned physician, who will be at hand at all times from then on to alleviate your discomforts with other drugs."

"I see," said Et. The words stuck in his throat. "I'll be under medication part of the time, then, once I'm confirmed as Et."

"All of the time," replied St. Onge, with a gentle smile.

Et nodded his head grimly.

"All right," he said. "It's a deal. I just want one thing."

"You're not in a position to make conditions," St. Onge said.

"Aren't I?" Et answered. "You wouldn't be going to this much trouble unless you wanted me pretty badly. I say, I want one thing."

"All right, let's hear it then," said St. Onge. "But it's going to have to be something within the regulations."

"It is," said Et. "But it's also protection for me. When the

Section Chiefs of the Earth Council—how many are there?"

"The Chiefs of Sections?" St. Onge said. "Eighteen."

"When they agree that I'm R-Master Etter Ho, I want to be there. I want to be there, physically, in the room with them, so that I can hear them say I'm R-Master Etter Ho. And I want the whole meeting a matter of public record. If something goes wrong later on, at least I'll know it wasn't because one of them thought it was safe to back out of the matter."

"What you're asking just can't be done," said Cele, speaking for the first time. "They hold their meetings by phone."

"Always?" demanded Et. "I heard—not always."

Cele said nothing.

"Almost always," said St. Onge. "In special cases they all meet together, physically, in one room. But there are still enough fanatics in the world to make a meeting like that dangerous. I don't think I can promise you that."

"Then I can't promise you anything," said Et. He laughed. "You're forgetting I'm already at the bottom. How much have I got to lose by not going along with you? I've got to have some reason to trust you—you and all of them—or it's no good."

St. Onge stood for a moment.

"All right," he said, then. "You'll meet them all, in the flesh, in one room. After all, this is a situation with serious ramifications."

He headed toward the door of the room. Cele followed him.

"Wait a minute!" Et called after them. "You can't just go off like that and leave me here, dangling. How long before I have this hearing? A month, a couple of weeks—?"

St. Onge stopped and looked back. He smiled oddly.

"Why keep you waiting that long?" St. Onge said. "Let's say tomorrow—twelve hours from now, Hong Kong time."

16

Et sat where he was, counting the seconds, until St. Onge and Cele had been gone long enough to get them to the entrance of the hotel and outside. Then he got up and went to the phone in his room and punched out the number of a local bookstore.

After a second the face of a young Oriental girl appeared on the screen.

"I'm at the Hotel Oceania," Et said. "The name is Wallace Ho. Do you have some kind of information book on R-Masters you could send over to me right now?"

"Right now?" The smooth, Oriental, almost childish face stared at him out of the screen. This was an emergency contact. Rico had set up at least one such for him in each city he was to stop in overnight on his way to Hong Kong.

"Right now," said Et. "Twelve hours from now I won'< be here any longer. I won't have any need for it."

"Twelve hours?"

"That's right."

"Let me see what I can do, please, sir."

"Thanks." Et punched off. Just in case there should, in defiance of regulations, be some kind of human or mechanical eye observing him, he went to the bar of the room, made himself a drink, and carried it back to his chair by the phone. But he only pretended to sip at it.

It was nearly four hours before the phone rang.

"Last copy of such was sold to a lady in your hotel," said the face from the bookstore. "She will lend it to you, though. Now down in lobby, checking out. If you go down, she will lend you the copy."

"Thanks," said Et.

He left the room and took the nearest elevator shaft down to the central main lobby of the hotel. There were perhaps half a hundred people milling about, and he suddenly realized that he had been given no description of the "lady" he was supposed to meet. Then common sense came to his rescue. He found a seat among a group of comfortable grav floats in a gardenlike secluded corner of the lobby and sat down to wait.

A few minutes later, a somewhat stiff-moving but slim-bodied elderly Occidental woman walked into the same area and took a seat opposite him. He looked into the woman's face and under the lines of makeup recognized Maea.

"Mr. Ho?" said Maea, in a filtered voice.

"Yes."

"My bookstore told me you very much wished to read a copy of a book I have; evidently I bought the last one they had in stock." She passed the small brown film card case to him. "Here you are."

"Thanks," he said.

She leaned forward and lowered her voice.

"What is it?" she murmured.

"Things have gone well," he said. "St. Onge took the bait, just as I told Rico he would. They're going to give me the chance to switch from Wally Ho to Etter Ho, but—" He told her about his conversation with St. Onge and Cele.

"So," he wound up, "I'm to be taken to meet the Earth Council's Section Chiefs tomorrow. And Rico told me it would take two weeks to make even the first two thousand doses of R-50. The rest of you'd probably all better split up and try to hide out."

"We couldn't hide long," she said, a little bitterly.

"What are you doing in this, anyway? Rico, Carwell, the makeup man, and I were supposed to be the only ones in on this part of it."

"The makeup man was a Mogow," she said. "Of course he came to me. Et"—she reached out to put her hand on his—"we haven't been really honest with you. You see, there's an organization within an organization, a special group in the Mogows that believes in getting results any way we can. I'm one of them; so was Wally. Our group had done some research with R-47 and thought we'd found an improved version of it. The physician at the clinic who treated Wally was a Mogow. He gave him what we thought was our improved version of the drug. But it wasn't—improved. It ruined him instead of making him an R-Master, the way we'd hoped."

He stared at her.

"Why didn't you tell me this before?" he asked.

"I'm sorry; we didn't trust you. You'd done nothing but idle your whole life away. We couldn't believe you could really change overnight into someone who wanted to help cure this sick world. I believed that about you, too" —she bit her lip—"until just last week. I deliberately got Al to talk about you. One night on your boat."

"Oh," said Et.

She looked at him curiously but went on.

"Al gave us a lot better picture of you than we'd been able to get before. You really were like Wally all along, only you took it out in pretending you didn't care about anything serious. When I was sure of that, I went to Rico and told him about myself and everything else. But by that time you'd already gone off as Wally."

"All right," he said. "That's good to know. But it doesn't change things. In twelve hours I meet the Section Chiefs, and according to what Rico told me there's no R-50 at all."

"There's a test run they made. Fifty doses, maybe. But who knows if it's right? Who knows if it'll work?"

He grinned a little wryly.

"Wally and I had a great-grandfather who was a missionary," he said. "Great-grandfather Bruder. He had a line for something like this: *'Not in my time, O Lord, but in thine.'* "

He stood up.

"Well, let's try it," he said. "Get back to Rico and tell him to go ahead. You'd better get away from me now, before you attract the wrong kind of attention to yourself."

She stood up also. They shook hands.

"Thank you very much for the book," he said loudly. "I'll send it back to you just as soon as I'm through."

"Take your time," she said and went off into the crowd of the lobby. He turned and went back up to his suite, to lie down on his bed. Surprisingly, sleep came easily to him, and he slept until he was wakened.

Two armed Field Examiners from the Auditor Corps came for him at three in the morning, Hong Kong time. They took him to an intercontinental and lifted him over the bulge of the world into late afternoon, landing him in the gray complex of EC administrative buildings in Halifax, Nova Scotia.

There he was stripped, showered, irradiated, and generally searched. He was re-dressed in a loose suit of gray coveralls and taken onward by the two Field Examiners.

By slideways and tunnels over some distance they conducted him at last to an unremarkable-looking conference room with a horseshoe table capable of seating perhaps twenty-five people. He was given a chair near the open end of the horseshoe and left to wait with one Field Examiner standing behind him on guard.

Some minutes went by with nothing happening. Then people began to trickle into the room—mostly middle-aged or older men and women—and take chairs around the horseshoe. Wilson, Patrick St. Onge's boss and the Accounting Section Chief, was the only one Et recognized immediately. Some of the others he recognized more slowly as EC Section Chiefs whose images he had seen in the news releases. Patrick St. Onge came in, glanced at Et, and went out again, not bothering this time to make any pretense of apology for the fact that a citizen had been brought in under guard by Field Examiners.

Around the table, those who had already seated themselves were chatting with their neighbors. There was a relaxed air as if this was very much a part of the ordinary day's routine. But the room was filling up rapidly. St. Onge came back in, followed by Cele, but they did not take seats. Nearly all the other seats were filled. The one in the very center of the upper curve of the horseshoe remained empty until two people, Wilson and a tall bony woman in her forties, both came up to it. They talked for a second, flipped a coin, and Wilson retired. The bony woman sat down in the center seat and reached for a gavel lying within reach. She rapped on the table.

Conversation died away around the room.

"All right," said the bony woman. "Saya Sorenson of Medical presiding at this policy meeting—this for the record. Everyone present? Yes, I see you all are. Now, Patrick?"

"With the permission of the Section Chiefs," Patrick St. Onge said, advancing into the open end of the horseshoe, "I've asked that today's policy meeting be an in-person one because we've been concerned lately with a possible abuse of the R-47 situation, in particular the making of R-Masters—"

"Excuse me, Patrick," broke in Wilson. "Perhaps we could have identification first?" He glanced at Et. "This, as I remember, is our latest Master, Etter Ho?"

"That," said St. Onge, "is something I intended to ask the Section Chiefs to decide. He's either Etter Ho or a conspirator against the regulations—or possibly both. But there are some other possible conspirators against the regulations involved in this situation. If I might bring them in now?"

"Go ahead," said Saya Sorenson.

There was a sound behind Et, and he turned to see the door opening and several Field Inspectors ushering in the coveralled figures of Maea and Carwell. After a second, a fourth figure was ushered in, to stand by the wall. Et's heart jumped in his chest. The fourth person was Wally, also in coveralls. He walked as Et had walked, and when they stopped him he folded his arms and looked down thoughtfully, as if abstracted from what was going on around him. There was no sign that the Field Examiners had yet realized that he was nothing more than a trained body. There was a little murmur around the table as the Section Chiefs looked from Wally to Et and back again.

"A remarkable resemblance," Saya Sorenson said. "For the record, Patrick, are they twins?"

"No, doctor," said Patrick. "Only brothers."

"Continue, then."

"Thank you. These four," said St. Onge, "together with one other—the secretary assigned by EC to Etter Ho, one Rico Erm—have possibly been engaged in a conspiracy to replace Etter Ho, a legitimate R-Master, with his brother Wallace, whom the Auditor Corps believes to be the man standing against the wall over there."

"Very interesting," said a young, slightly heavy woman with lank hair and a heavy jaw. "But—"

Saya Sorenson rapped with her gavel.

"If Social Control will reserve comments until later?" she said.

"I had a point to make that was pertinent," protested the younger woman.

"I support Nicolina Drega," said Wilson. "Let her speak."

"Call for a vote, then," said Saya Sorenson, "since Accounting evidently wants us to be here until midnight. A simple majority is all that's required. All in favor of Social Control Section Chief Nicolina Drega speaking at this point, raise their hand."

Hands went up.

"Passed. The floor is yours, Nicolina."

"I was going to say," said the younger woman, "the supposition is too farfetched. It would be impossible to substitute an ordinary citizen even for another ordinary citizen, let alone for an R-Master."

"We have evidence that the security of the zero-zero files has been breached," said St. Onge. "There is a possibility it was this group which attempted to exchange identity records of the two brothers. At the moment an identity check supports the man against the wall as Wallace, not Etter, Ho, but we believe this to be so only because the conspirators failed to achieve the exchange they planned."

"If the zero-zero files prove him to be the rightful R-Master," said a fat man on the far side of Saya Sorenson, "what's all the fuss about? Speaking for Special Services, I propose we confirm the seated man as Master Ho, deal with the others as criminals according to whatever regulations apply, and move along." He looked around the table.

"If that is the opinion of the Section Chiefs," said St. Onge. "In the name of the regulations, however, I wished to point out that the security of the zero-zero files may have been breached, a breach stemming from a possible breaking of regulations."

"Oh, come now, Patrick, we don't need all that," said the fat man. "Naturally, none of us is going to bend, let alone break, regulations."

"In that I agree with Special Services," said Nicolina. "We've got more important things to do, with a world to run, than to sit in judgment on petty criminal cases."

"But," said Wilson, "is this merely a petty criminal case? It deals with a possible zero-zero file breach plus an attempt to impersonate an R-Master. The Section Chiefs of this council may remember that Accounting—over strong objections by Medical—first insisted on setting Patrick St. Onge, here, to keep an eye on this Etter Ho, once he was made an R-Master. Fortunately, a majority of the council backed us in the decision to do just that, or this present situation might never have been uncovered."

"And I was saying I doubted that—doubted it profoundly," Saya Sorenson said dryly. "Accounting, you are ruled out of order. It happens that in this case the Auditor Corps has let the wool be pulled over its eyes to a shocking extent; if it were not for the alertness of an investigative branch of our own Medical personnel—"

"Investigative branch? What investigative branch?" Wilson was pounding the table with his fist. "Since when has Medical been concerned with EC security? This is a matter that has been thrashed out in this council before. The Auditor Corps and the Auditor Corps alone is authorized to guard the regulations that preserve our utopian Earth—"

"And it's precisely because they've been doing such a bad job of it that Medical has had to take steps on its own—for which the council will be thankful, once it learns the facts," retorted Saya. "The Auditor Corps observed the operation of a Mogow militant unit right under its nose without suspecting anything. Only the superior loyalty of our regular Medical personnel allowed our section to be alerted."

She turned to look at the back wall against which Wally, Maea, and Carwell were standing.

"Dr. Carwell," Saya said. "Will you tell the council what you know and what you did?"

Morgan Carwell rolled forward, clumsy as a bear.

"I'm a physician at an R-47 clinic," he said earnestly to the faces around the large table. "I have to admit I was a Mogow too, for a while. But I became convinced there was more harm than good to be accomplished in that direction. There was another physician at the clinic who, like me, belonged to that subversive organization. For Mogow purposes he experimented on his own to improve the R-47 formula. Then he tried out the result of that amateurish experimentation on a young man, a Mogow from another branch of the organization, who came to the clinic deliberately to act as guinea pig for him. The result was that the young man suffered an extreme negative reaction to the drug."

He turned and pointed to Wally, still standing against the wall, arms folded, gazing at the floor as if lost in thought.

"It was that young man there," he said. There was a murmur from the room.

"What—" began Nicolina.

The gavel banged down.

"Order. Let him finish. Go on, doctor," said Saya Sorenson.

"So I reported the whole matter to my Medical superiors and promised to do whatever I could to stop such deadly experimentation in the future. Later on, when Etter Ho asked me to be his personal physician, I checked with my Medical superiors and they asked me to accept the post and keep them informed of what went on with this new R-Master, since there was some suspicion he had been connected, like his brother, with the Mogows."

Carwell stopped and wiped his forehead, which was gleaming with sweat.

"I did," he said. "I found out much more than the auditors did. The man sitting is actually Etter Ho. The one standing is Wallace Ho, a revived cryogenic, who actually has no mind or personality. He's been response-trained to play Etter's role, while Etter, with the Mogows, tried to discover some fanciful hidden research concerning a developed and improved form of R-47. They believed they'd found it; I understand they were going to try to duplicate this supposed improved form of the drug with the facilities of a laboratory set up underneath the home of Lee Malone, another R-Master—"

"What? When?" snapped Wilson. "Patrick, order Field Examiners to Lee Malone's immediately—"

"It's not necessary," interrupted Saya. "Our own people have already raided the place. But the laboratory equipment has been cleaned out. Lee Malone is missing, along with your Rico Erm."

"Erm?" Wilson stared.

"Exactly," said Saya icily. "One of your most trusted secretaries, I think? I should, by the way, reassure the council. There is no need for worry about any of this. We of Medical have allowed it to run on this long only in order to demonstrate how badly Accounting and its parasecurity arm, the Auditor Corps, have been serving us all. The time has long been past when each section should maintain its own security force. Never mind that now however. The point is that Medical—not Accounting—has had this little Mogow conspiracy under control from the very beginning. Let me tell you—"

"This is outrageous!" Wilson lifted his voice. "Medical is violating all the rules of order of this—"

"Quiet," said the fat man. "I want to hear this." There

was a chorus of agreement from the other figures around the table. "Go on, Saya."

"Gladly. As I was saying, we've had the conspiracy under control from the inside all the time the Auditor Corps was watching it and worrying about it from the outside. The injection of Wallace Ho with an experimental version of R-47 raised the possibility that more efforts like this might well be made by irresponsible private groups in the future. If so, how should they be controlled? We at Medical evolved a plan for control and proceeded to test it, in this case. Wallace Ho had inadvertently been made a near-idiot—or would have been, if he had not committed suicide before the process had taken its full effect. To smoke out the conspirators who had been involved in producing the drug used on him, we offered them a bait. When Wallace's brother Etter decided to take the R-47 treatment, we saw that he was given not R-47—"

"Not the R-50!" cried Nicolina. "You didn't break the council commitment against using the final form of the drug!"

"No, no, of course not," said Saya. "We merely used a slightly more advanced form, the R-48c. It was sufficient to ensure Etter an R-Master development but still left him in need of palliative medication."

"Which he refused to take!" snapped Wilson.

"Well, yes, that's true," said Saya, glancing at Et in the chair. "He did refuse all medication. But that was a minor matter. As we suspected, the Mogows and even some others like your Rico Erm, who were at heart subversives, took the bait and gathered around him in hopes of making some profound alteration in our system. As a result, we uncovered a number of most dangerous people; not only that, we will continue to uncover more as Lee Malone and Rico Erm, in their flight, lead us to others as they turn to them for shelter and help."

"Meanwhile," Wilson ground out, "Malone and Erm will be turning out doses of R-50 by the hundreds, if not thousands."

"Which need not worry us," said Saya. "An R-Master, whether produced with R-47 or R-50, is still nothing more than a highly effective problem-solving human entity. He or she is effective only in proportion to the power he or she already possesses. It goes without saying that the Mogows are, almost without exception, outside the working system of the EC; it's with the EC—with us—that the real power lies. The R-Masters produced by Malone and Erm may be somewhat troublesome to us for a short while, but there's little major change they can accomplish before they betray themselves into our hands. Bear in mind that the EC is a system of world management employing millions of people. What can a few thousand, working from the outside, do against anything so massive?"

"By God!" said Wilson. "You take it calmly enough!"

Saya shrugged.

"I leave it to the other Section Chiefs of this council to decide—by vote—if I'm not right," she said. "Shall we vote on it?"

"By all means," said the fat man, glancing at his chronometer. "I have a dinner engagement. . . ."

There was a mutter of approval around the table.

"You're a bunch of idiots!" exploded Wilson. "Idiots, playing with matches in a fireworks factory!"

"Be quiet and vote," Saya told him. "No one here is about to be worried by your dire predictions."

"How about mine?" said Et.

His voice brought heads from around the council table to look at him.

"Keep him quiet, you Field Examiners," commanded Saya brusquely.

"Stop and think," said Et. "Not everyone wants to be an R-Master—"

The rest of his words were lost as one of the Field Examiners by him got an arm around his neck from behind, choking him.

"Let him talk," said Wilson malevolently.

"Yes," said Nicolina. "That was rather an interesting start he made there. Let him talk."

"Let go!" snapped Wilson directly to the Field Examiner. "That's an order—from me!"

The Field Examiner let go. Et massaged his throat for a moment and got his voice back into working order.

"I was going to point out something," he said. "Not everyone wants to be an R-Master, even if the chance is given to them. Some people don't want to spend their lives being high-powered puzzle-solvers. Others have personal reasons"—he looked around the table—"like all of you here have."

"Shut him up!" snapped Saya.

"I figured out quite a while ago why none of you took advantage of the R-50," Et said. "It was part of the business of not rocking the boat, of not risking anyone getting an edge over everyone else. I'll bet you all take monthly or even daily examinations to prove there's no R-50 serum in you. Aren't I right?"

None of them answered.

"Of course I'm right," said Et swiftly. "That's the one thing you overlooked in letting Malone and Rico Erm get away with the means to make the R-50. The one group of people who'd really threaten the EC system if they were R-Masters are you people here."

"There's no danger of that," said Saya. "Do you think we're going to invite Malone in to treat us all?"

"Not Malone," said Et. "Someone else. . . . Wally! *Now!*"

At the end of the line of people against the wall of the room, Wally moved, in the last of his trained movements. His face had no expression, but his hand went to his neck and grabbed. The skin there opened as if it were cloth, fitted with a pocket. Inside was a small metal capsule. Before any of the Field Examiners nearby could reach him, Wally took it in his fingers and tossed it onto the floor in the center of the horseshoe table.

It exploded.

Suddenly, the room was obscured by an eye-stinging mist. Sitting at the table, Et felt as if the whole place moved about him. He started to fall and clutched at the edge of the table to hold on, but his fingers had no strength. His mind was spinning. The mist began to thin, and the clearing lights of the room hurt his eyes. The sound of voices roared and thundered in his ears, so exaggeratedly loud that he could not make sense of what was being said.

Now it was clear enough to see that Wally had fallen. He lay face down and still. Near him Maea and Carwell looked different. Their faces were changed. No, thought Et, not their faces, just their expressions, the way they were looking at things. Had he looked like that, he wondered, in that first moment at the clinic when the advanced form of R-47 had taken effect? Or was R-50 more potent that way?

But he had no time to puzzle over such things. Around

the room, they were all changing—Maea, St. Onge, Wilson, Carwell, Nicolina, all of them. Et's strength was almost gone. Whatever hammer blow came from the basic drug of which R-47 and R-50 were variants, a double dose in a single individual was overwhelming. But it did not matter now.

His fingers slipped. In spite of his effort to hold himself upright, he fell forward on the table, its smooth surface against his cheek. Someone was bending over him. It was Maea.

"Not in my time, O Lord, but in thine," said the voice of Great-grandfather Bruder somewhere nearby, and the phrase had a sound like trumpets.

The light was becoming too much for him. It hurt his eyes. He closed his lids against it, and there opened before him a world—no, a universe—made available by the R-50, a universe in shape and distance, depth and content such as no one had ever imagined before. He had won.

17

The *Sarah* swayed slightly to the tropical Pacific swell, under the stars. The ship was almost becalmed, and the ocean was strangely smooth. The dark threads of sea snakes writhed in the moonlight on the glinting surface of the water.

Al was down in the cabin with a light on over his bunk, reading. Undisturbed by that light, up in the cockpit of the sloop, Et and Maea had the vessel, the sea, and the stars to themselves.

". . . and there's the Southern Cross," Et was saying.

"How strange," Maea said. "I've seen it before, but right now it's like looking at it for the first time."

"And there's Alpha Centauri," Et said. He was half sitting, half lying on the cushions of the stern seat with Maea on his right side and the rim of the wheel under his left hand. He could have roped the wheel but he liked the feel of it, alive under his fingers, as the boat eased into every little breath of air.

"Where?" asked Maea.

"See, one of the pointers, there, for the Crux—the Southern Cross. See it now?"

"Yes," said Maea. "Do you think we'll ever go there?"

"Why not?" said Et and grinned at the night. "Now that we're starting to get the world moving forward again."

She shivered slightly.

"You're so sure," she said. "You're sure about every-thing—that the bureaucracy'll go smash, that a better kind of society'll be born—you're even sure *we're* safe."

"Of course we're safe," he said. "I explained that to you."

"Tell me again. I feel better, hearing the way you say it."

"Why, just as I told you," Et said. "We're counters, you and I—particularly me. If I'd died after that double dose of R-drugs, none of them would have missed me. But since I didn't die, maybe I'm supervaluable. Who knows?"

"Are you supervaluable?"

"I don't know!" Et laughed. "I couldn't feel any differ-ent when I had one R-47 dose inside me. I still don't feel any different with that plus the R-50. Maybe I can turn the universe inside out—but what good does the ability do me if I don't know I have it?"

"Be serious."

"I am serious," he said. "Well, almost serious. All right, seriously, no, I don't think that second dose did anything except make me a little more resistant to the side-effects, the aches and pains I'd been stuck with as a result of the first dose. But what does that matter? The point is I might be valuable. And none of the R-Masters we now have as Section Chiefs are going to risk destroying something valuable. By the same token, each one's watching every other one to make sure that none of the others tries to make use of me. So . . . standoff. They all leave me alone."

"And me alone?" she asked.

"And you. And Al." Et nodded toward the lighted cabinway forward. "We're a package. So here we are, free to do what we want."

"But what makes you so sure they'll tear each other apart, the way you think they will?"

"Not tear each other apart," said Et. "Eat each other up—like the gingham dog and the calico cat."

"What's that?"

"You don't know that old poem by Eugene Field?" He quoted:

> "The gingham dog and the calico cat,
> Side by side on the table sat,
> 'Twas half past twelve, and (what do you think?)
> Neither one nor t'other had slept a wink.
> The old Dutch clock and the Chinese plate
> Appeared to know as sure as fate
> There was going to be a terrible spat . . .

". . . and so it goes for three or four more verses like that," Et said. "But then it winds up:

> "Next morning where the two had sat
> They found no trace of dog or cat;
> And some folks think unto this day
> That burglars stole that pair away!
> But the truth about that cat and pup
> Is this: they ate each other up.

"Which," said Et, "is what our EC Section Chiefs are going to do to themselves and to the EC bureaucracy. You see, they were wiser than they thought, in all leaving R-50 alone. They made things work by everyone agreeing to play by the rules. But it was easy to play by the rules when they were ordinary—even mediocre—men and women."

"And now they're not?"

"Now they're stuck with minds that can see too many ways of playing the angles and cutting the corners. They've got the problem-solving minds of R-Masters and R-Masters' compulsion to use that ability. They may hold the line, for a while, and keep on playing by the rules. But sooner or later—probably already—one or the other of them is going to take an unorthodox route to some end he particularly wants, and just as soon as one of the others suspects—even suspects—that a fellow Section Chief is breaking the rules, he or she's going to begin breaking them also to keep even. Result: the gingham dog and the calico cat syndrome."

"But that doesn't destroy the system."

"Don't forget," said Et. "This is crumbling the pyramid from the top down. These people control the system. Big chunks of it. They'll end up using those chunks in rule-breaking ways and taking the chunks along with them into battle with each other. In the end, the whole hierarchy will break up into anarchy. Meanwhile, the R-50 that Lee and Rico will be making will be spreading and increasing the new crop of independent problem-solvers on the outside, ready to take over when the original system crumbles."

"Oh, I believe that," said Maea pensively. "After all, I'm an R-Master myself now, too. I can believe in things crumbling. But what's to say they'll ever be put back together again?"

"We're a technological society," Et said. "We need order and law. Besides, remember, not everybody wants to be an R-Master."

She looked at him doubtfully in the moonlight.

"What makes you so sure about that?"

He grinned at her and then turned to shout down the companionway to the cabin.

"Al!"

"What?" Al's voice came back.

"How about we get some R-50 and make you an R-Master too, next stop we make?"

"Go to hell!"

"Al," shouted Et, "you don't mean that!"

"The hell I don't!" Al's voice was positive. "That's for the rest of you. The earth, the sea, and me—we like ourselves just the way we are."

"You see," said Et, more quietly to Maea, "why I wanted to keep Al out of the council room that day. He was my touchstone. You and I—the bright ones, the flaky ones, the earth-shakers—we show up and disappear. Al stays on forever, generation after generation, and produces more like us when he needs us."

She did not say anything for a moment.

"You don't like the way we are, then?" she said, not looking at him.

"Of course I do," he answered. "But that's the kind of a human critter I am—and the kind you are. Al's a different kind, and there's more like him than there are like you and me."

"What's the use of civilization, then?" she said. "What's the use of anything? If it isn't becoming better thinkers that we're after, what is it?"

"I don't know," he said. "How can I tell? I'm a man of

my time, just like you're a woman of your—of our time. But I can guess that the R-whatever drugs, and everything else like them, aimed at making us smarter, may turn out to lead us down a blind alley."

"What makes you think so?" she said. "As I say, if being smarter isn't what we're after, what is?"

"And I say," he said, "I don't know what is. But there's lots of things brains can't do for you. All the intelligence in the world won't help you build a boat like this one, until you've learned the craft of boatbuilding from the keel up. Being very smart doesn't automatically make you paint a better picture or compose a better piece of music. The best you can say for intelligence is that it helps you along the road toward the things you want. But the things themselves—the actual things—have to be something more than just intelligence products."

There was a moment's silence between them. Then she spoke.

"There's children," she said. "The next generation."

He looked at her quizzically through the darkness.

"Already," he said, "you're bringing that topic into the conversation."

"It never was out," she said. "Everything else in the world and time adds up to it."